The Two Sanibel Sunset Detectives

Also by Ron Base

Fiction

Matinee Idol

Foreign Object

Splendido

Magic Man

The Strange

The Sanibel Sunset Detective

The Sanibel Sunset Detective Returns

Another Sanibel Sunset Detective

Non-fiction

The Movies of the Eighties (with David Haslam)

If the Other Guy Isn't Jack Nicholson, I've Got the Part

Marquee Guide to Movies on Video

Cuba Portrait of an Island (with Donald Nausbaum)

www.ronbase.com

Read Ron's blog at

www.ronbase.wordpress.com

Contact Ron at

ronbase@ronbase.com

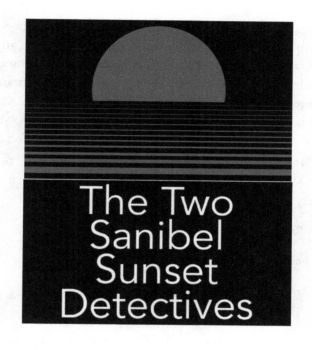

The Two Sanibel Sunset Detectives

a novel by

RON BASE

West-End Books

Library and Archives Canada Cataloguing in Publication

Base, Ron, 1948-, author

    The Two Sanibel Sunset Detectives / Ron Base.

ISBN 978-0-9736955-7-1 (pbk.)
    I. Title.

PS8553.A784T86 2013   C813'.54   C2013-907231-4

West-End Books
80 Front St. East, Suite 605
Toronto, Ontario
Canada M5E 1T4

Cover design: Brian Frommer
Text design: Ric Base
Electronic formatting: Ric Base
Sanibel Island map: Anna Kornuta

First Edition

For the real Joshua and Madison.
Thanks for lending your names to the story.
And also for Nathan and Cohen.
Four wondrous grandchildren who
complete my life.

Of course there are these unique islands called Sanibel and Captiva. And Fort Myers is in fact right across the causeway. And yes, the Sanibel-Captiva Chamber of Commerce Visitors Center exists, as do any number of the other places named in the novel. But there is no Dayton's on Sanibel, and there is no Traven mansion, either. Please keep in mind this is a work of fiction, and none of the situations or characters described in the story exist. Well, okay, there really was an Elvis Presley—although sometimes you do wonder.

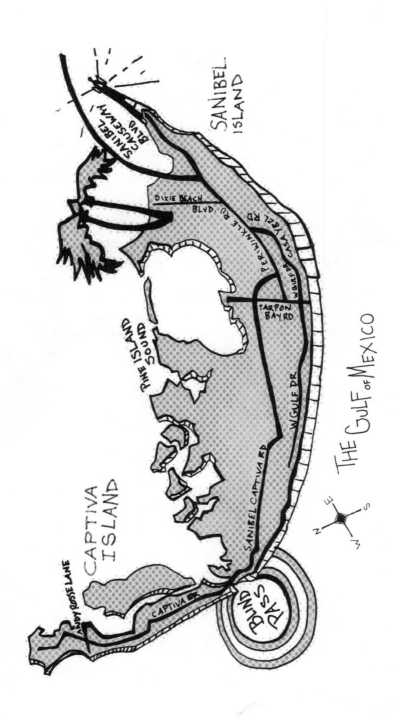

One

Elvis was singing "Follow That Dream," Tree Callister backing the King on rhythm guitar, when the Sanibel Island police pulled him over.

Tree could not think why he kept imagining himself playing the guitar with Elvis seeing as how he had no idea how to play the guitar. He also had no idea why the police would stop him since his battered old Volkswagen Beetle convertible was only going about twenty-five miles per hour along Periwinkle Way.

Elvis finished singing and Tree's guitar playing faded. He forced himself back to reality, watching in the Beetle's rear view mirror as the officer left his vehicle. For a moment, the officer disappeared from sight, but then he loomed at the driver's side.

"Morning," the police officer said. His head was shaved and he seemed to burst from his uniform, as if his muscles and his girth were too much to be contained by mere clothing. He wore wrap-around sunglasses that gave him a certain distanced, mechanical quality. It was as though Tree had been stopped by Robocop.

"What's the problem, officer?" Tree asked, a question repeated by suspected miscreants like himself across America this morning.

"Show me your license and registration please," the officer said.

Tree fumbled in his wallet while the officer tilted his head away, as if his attention had been caught by something much more important.

It had been so long since anyone had asked him for his driver's license, Tree had trouble finding it, and when he did, it refused to come out of the plastic holder in his wallet. "The damn thing's stuck," Tree said.

"Take your time, sir," the officer said, keeping his gaze averted.

Tree finally pried the license loose and handed it along with the registration—which he found at the bottom of the glove compartment—to the officer. That caused the officer to shift his gaze and idly inspect the paperwork in his hand. "You're Walter Tremain Callister?"

Tree didn't like to be called Walter. He gritted his teeth. "Yes."

"Hold on a minute, Walter," the officer said, and without waiting for a reply disappeared from view. Tree craned around and watched him saunter back to his cruiser, hips rolling. On the radio Stevie Wonder sang "You Are the Sunshine of My life." No sunshine so far this morning. He drummed his fingers against the steering wheel. The officer reappeared at the driver's side. "Walter, step out of the car, please."

"What?" Tree jerked in surprise.

"Step out of the car, please."

"You've got to be kidding. What's wrong?"

"Walter," the officer said, "don't make me ask you again. Step out of the vehicle."

Tree opened the door and eased himself stiffly from the Beetle. He was taller than the Robocop Sanibel police officer. But not by much. As Tree faced him, the officer took a step back in case Tree tried to go for the gun he must have suspected was hidden in his cargo shorts.

"What I need you to do, Walter, I need you to move back to the cruiser."

Tree forced himself to tamp down his rising anger. "What's wrong?" he said. "I have a right to know why you're doing this."

"I'm asking you to move back to the cruiser, Walter," the cop said. "I need you to co-operate."

Tree went back to the cruiser, the officer following, keeping his distance. "Now, Walter, I want you to turn around and face the cruiser, and spread your hands on the hood."

"You're kidding," Tree said.

The officer did not smile when he said, "Yeah kidding, Walter. I joke around like this every morning. So humor me and spread your hands on the hood."

Tree sighed and did as he was told, bending over, spreading his legs, and placing his hands against the warm metal of the cruiser. From behind him, he heard the officer say, "Are you carrying a weapon, Walter?"

"My name's not Walter," Tree said.

"Are you carrying a weapon, Walter?"

"No," Tree said.

"Okay, Walter, I'm going to pat you down."

Tree felt the officer's hands on his shoulders, big meaty paws moving down his body, whacking away at his rib cage, pulling at his T-shirt, ensuring there was no gun shoved into the waistband of his shorts. When he finished, the officer said, "Okay, you can straighten up now, Walter.

Tree removed his hands from the car, and turned toward the officer who once again had backed off a few paces. On Periwinkle, traffic was slowing so that the tourists could get a better look at the spectacle.

"What's this all about?" Tree said.

"Don't move, Walter," the officer replied.

Presently, a brown Buick approached and turned onto the road shoulder, parking a few feet behind the cruiser.

The driver's door opened, and a handsome young man stepped out. The sun glistened against Detective Owen Markfield's smooth, tanned skin. It glinted off the shiny perfection of his blond-streaked hair, artfully combed back from a high, wrinkle-free forehead. Markfield, in a blue-striped Tommy Bahama shirt, wearing Margarita loafers, was camera-ready for the Sanibel Island Detective TV series he already appeared to be starring in. But then Tree got a look at the smile on Markfield's face, and he knew the detective could never be the hero of any TV series. With that smile, Owen Markfield could only be the villain.

"Tree Callister," Markfield said in a voice edged with a sneer.

"I should have known you were behind this," Tree said.

"You've met Officer T. J. Hanks," Markfield said.

"We were just getting to know each other," Tree said.

"T.J. is one of Sanibel Island's most talented and dedicated policemen. He may also be the toughest mother in South Florida. I've been filling in Officer Hanks, telling him about your background, the fact that you are a suspected killer and a thief who has stolen—what? Nine million dollars?"

Tree addressed Officer Hanks. "Detective Markfield has an exaggerated view of me. I don't kill people and I don't have nine million dollars."

Officer Hanks gave him a blank stare.

Markfield stepped so close, Tree could smell the expensive after shave recently applied to that smooth, tanned jaw. His eyes had gone dead. And he barely moved his lips when he said, "You are a lying son of a bitch. If you didn't kill the woman I loved, you were certainly responsible for her death, and then you stole that money, and now I am bound and determined you are going to pay for it."

Officer Hanks added, "I don't like killers and I don't like thieves."

"There you go, Tree," Markfield said, regaining his smile as he moved away. "Officer Hanks doesn't like killers and thieves. That's why Officer Hanks is going to help me bring you down."

"I wouldn't have thought you needed any help," Tree managed to say.

Markfield just grinned his TV villain-of-the-week grin. "I thought the two of you should meet, so you could have some idea of what you're up against."

"I'm shaking in my boots." Tree tried to make it sound as though he was being sarcastic. In fact, he was shaking in his boots.

Markfield's grin only widened. "You know what, Tree? I think you are."

2

I was in *G.I. Blues* with Elvis," Rex Baxter was saying. Dapper this morning in a loose-fitting crimson shirt and white linen pants, tanned and fit having lately shed twenty pounds, Rex leaned against the edge of the stage at the Big Arts Center talking to a handsome blond-haired man who appeared to hang on Rex's every word. Exactly what Rex liked.

"Isn't that something?" said the blond-haired man with Rex. "Elvis, huh? You were actually in a movie with Elvis?"

"I played the role of Captain Hobart," Rex said.

"It's been so long since I've seen the movie," said the blond-haired man. "What was he like? Elvis, I mean."

Tree had heard the story before. Tree had heard all Rex's stories as they had been friends since their Chicago days when Tree was a young *Sun-Times* reporter, and Rex hosted an afternoon TV show. This was after Rex spent years in Hollywood doing bit parts in movies, although, if you listened to Rex, there were no bit parts, at least not that he played. The beloved president of the Sanibel-Captiva Chamber of Commerce was very much the star of his own life.

"Elvis had just been released from the army, a nice, courteous kid, a real gentleman," Rex said, ignoring Tree's presence. "But he had about as much interest in acting as I have in flying to the moon. He and those guys he hung with—the Memphis Mafia as they were known—all they wanted to do was horse around in golf carts. Elvis was a whole lot more interested in Juliet Prowse, his co-star. She was engaged to Sinatra at the time, although I think she was up to a few things with Elvis."

"Juliet Prowse," the blond-haired man said. "Don't remember her."

"A dancer," Rex said. "She never amounted to much in the movies. But at least she concentrated when she was doing a scene."

"And Elvis didn't?"

"Something happened to him when he got in front of a camera. It was as if he wasn't there. He just shot through his lines, reciting them, skating along the surface."

"Those movies were pretty lousy," the blond-haired man said.

"But they were very popular," Rex said. "*G.I. Blues* was a big hit. Everyone loved Elvis back then, and, of course, he had that voice."

"Elvis," the blond-haired man said. "That's just so fascinating, Rex."

Rex beamed—until he noticed Tree and said, "It's a good thing you're just one of the acceptors this year. Otherwise I would be prepared to wring your neck for showing up so late."

"Sorry, Rex. I was unavoidably delayed."

"Our annual Academy Awards satire show is becoming a tradition here on Sanibel," Rex admonished. A tradition that dated back all of three years, but who was counting?

"The show only works because we all come together to make it work—and that means being on time for rehearsals."

"I understand," Tree said.

"Do you know what you're going to do on Oscar night?"

"Don't worry about a thing, Rex, I'm going to knock them dead," Tree promised. "You'll see. I've got quite a little presentation prepared."

"We've only got one more rehearsal, so you better come through," Rex said. He indicated the blond-haired man standing nearby. "I want you to meet the guy who's going to be presenting the Oscar to you. Tree Callister, Ryde Bodie."

Ryde was nearly as tall as Rex, athletic with startling blue eyes that complemented the blast furnace smile he delivered as the two men shook hands.

"Great to meet you," he said.

"Ryde?" Tree said.

"Short for Ryder," Ryde Bodie said. "What about you? What's Tree short for?"

"Tremain. But that was too much for anyone when I was a kid, so I got saddled with Tree."

Rex said, "Like I told you, Tree is Sanibel Island's only private detective."

Ryde Bodie looked at Tree in a different way. "You're a private detective?"

"That's right," Tree said, wishing Rex hadn't brought it up.

"A private detective on the island? Like Mike Hammer and Philip Marlowe, guys like that?"

"Only without the gun and the trench coat."

"No trench coat, huh?"

Tree said, "It's too hot for trench coats."

"How can you not have a gun?"

"Do you?" Tree shot back.

Ryde Bodie delivered another grin. "I'm not a private eye."

"Ryde's new to the island," Rex said.

"I love it here," Ryde said. "It's a perfect place to raise kids, don't you think? I mean, it's Florida's last untouched paradise. I looked all over for just the right spot, and this is it, no question. I suppose it gets busy with tourists in season, but so what? You can't do better than this, right, Tree? I mean you live here, too, don't you? On the island?"

"Tree's wife, Freddie, just bought Dayton's supermarket," Rex said helpfully.

Now Ryde Bodie regarded Tree with another look: impressed, this time. "You don't say? Dayton's? Your wife? Well that's something, isn't it? The private eye and the supermarket owner. There's a unique combination."

"Freddie doesn't actually own the store," Tree managed to interject. "She's part of a syndicate that's bought the five stores in the area."

"Yeah, but she's running the show, right? She's the boss lady, is she not? That's great. Admirable. Women are taking over the world, aren't they? Leaving us men in the dust. The way of the world, don't you think, Tree?"

"You may be right," Tree said.

Ryde Bodie gripped Tree's hand hard, a manly handshake. "Pleasure to meet you, Tree. Really. A private eye. Right here on Sanibel. We'll see more of each other, won't we? I mean we're in this Oscar thing together, right Rex?"

Rex said, "As long as everyone turns up for rehearsal on time."

"Hey, thanks for including me," Ryde said. "It's gonna be great fun."

He turned and swirled out the door, shirttail flapping behind him. "How did you meet him?" Tree asked.

Rex said, "At Dayton's, where else? He seems affable enough. And he's obviously got some money."

"If that's the criteria for being in the show," Tree said, "what am I doing here? I don't have any money at all."

"Hey, you get a pass."

"Because I've known you forever?"

"Because you give the rest of us something to talk about."

"I do? What do they talk about?"

"What you did with that nine million dollars."

"I don't have nine million dollars."

"But you'd tell your old pal, Rex if you had it, wouldn't you?"

Tree gave him a look. Rex pounced on it. "See? That's what's got everyone talking. You won't come right out and deny it."

"I just did. I don't have nine million dollars."

Rex said, "Just make sure you spend it right here on Sanibel. Don't go running off to the South of France and spending it there."

"You've got my word on that," Tree said.

———

Outside the Big Arts Center, Tree was still thinking about his encounter with Detective Owen Markfield and his pal, Officer T.J. Hanks, and how dumb he had been to even entertain the notion Markfield might leave him alone. This morning's confrontation was proof that the cop was not about to do anything of the sort.

"Hey, there," a voice called as Tree reached his Volkswagen Beetle. Tree turned to see Ryde Bodie pull up in a black Cadillac Escalade. "I thought that was you, Tree," Ryde said, leaning out the window. "Where are you headed? Off to do a little private detecting?"

No, Tree thought. I'm headed into the office to try to figure out how to get a vengeful cop off my back. But Mr.

Ryde Bodie behind the wheel of his Cadillac SUV doesn't have to know that.

"How about you, Ryde? What do you do here on the island?"

"On the island? On Sanibel I relax and raise two kids. This is my escape to paradise. The place where I chill out and recharge the batteries."

"Okay," Tree said. "What do you do when you're not on the island?"

Ryde Bodie grinned and said, "Off the island, I bring people together for everyone's mutual benefit."

"That's intriguingly vague," Tree said.

"Is it? Do you think it is? Well, it's not as intriguing as it sounds. It's kind of boring most of the time, actually. Finding one person with big money to invest and then finding another person with big money to invest and bringing them together to make even bigger money."

That still sounded vague to Tree, but he wasn't about to press it. "I'd better be getting to work," he said.

"Hey, Tree, we should keep in touch. You never know when I might need a private detective."

"Do you think you're going to need a private detective, Ryde?"

That induced another grin. "Like I say, you never know. Who knows they're going to need a detective, until they need a detective, right?"

Tree pulled out his wallet and handed Ryde his card. "Give me a call," Tree said.

"I might just surprise you," Ryde said as he drove off.

3

"Where's Rex?" Todd Jackson asked. He had dropped into Tree's office at the Chamber of Commerce Visitors Center for his morning coffee.

"He's still at the Big Arts Center."

"Is he doing that Oscar show again this year?"

"He's even got me involved in it," Tree said.

"I don't get that show at all," Todd said. An elegant man with a carefully trimmed moustache and an endless enthusiasm for everything, Todd ran a crime scene clean-up company called Sanibel Biohazard.

"It's going to be great," Tree said. "Did I ever tell you I once thought about becoming an actor?"

"Now that you've got nine million dollars you can do that," Todd said.

"Who says I have nine million dollars?"

"Rex."

"He really thinks I have that money?"

"He does. And he doesn't."

"What's that mean?"

"He believes, in general, you're too honest to steal, but then again, he suspects we are all susceptible when it comes to that kind of money. Even you."

Tree rolled his eyes.

Todd leaned forward in the chair fronting Tree's desk. "I'm still trying to get all this straight," he said. "Elizabeth Traven, the wife of the late, unlamented media mogul Brand Traven—the husband who she may or may not have murdered—hooks up with a group of former intelligence agents who rip off the president of Tajikistan to the tune of nine million dollars."

"Supposedly they ripped him off," Tree said.

"Then Elizabeth disappears and because you've done work for her before, these guys—the former intelligence agents—they hire you to find her."

"Correct."

"So you do find Elizabeth, but then she disappears again, and the next thing she turns up dead in Key West along with her two accomplices. In fact, just about everyone involved in this crazy scheme seems to have ended up dead. Everyone, that is, but you."

"That's because I wasn't part of it," Tree said. "I was only doing what I was hired to do—which was to find Elizabeth."

"But Detective Owen Markfield of the Sanibel Police Department thinks you're lying."

"Owen Markfield along with the police in Key West and the Lee County Sheriff's Department, as well as any number of other law enforcement agencies."

"But they have no proof."

"There is no proof."

"And therefore you are innocent."

"Let's just say I don't have nine million dollars," Tree amended.

"They found five hundred thousand dollars of the missing money in Key West, but they think there's more, right?"

"Elizabeth swore up and down the millions everyone was looking for never existed. At the time I thought she was lying, but it turns out she wasn't."

"The government of Tajikistan says there are millions."

"What do they know?" Tree said.

Todd shook his head. "I know a lot of the guys over at the Sanibel Police. They all think Markfield is an egotistical, self-promoting jerk. But nobody wants to get on the wrong side of him."

"I'm afraid it's too late for me," Tree said. "I'm already on his wrong side."

"My friend," Todd said. "You are in a manure wagon load of trouble."

"That much I've figured out," Tree said. "The part I'm having trouble with is how I get out of it."

"Give back the money?"

Tree groaned. "That puts us at square one. I *don't have* the money."

They were interrupted by the sound of footsteps coming up the stairs. They both turned as a small African American boy dressed in a T-shirt and shorts entered Tree's office.

"Marcello O'Hara," Tree said.

"Hey," Marcello said. "How you doing, man?"

Todd got to his feet, shook Marcello's hand, and said, "Good to see you. You've grown since the last time I saw you."

"I'm grown *up* now," Marcello said confidently.

"Is that so?" Todd said. "Well, I'll leave you two adults to it. I've got a crime scene over in Bonita Springs needs cleaning up. I'll talk to you later."

Todd sauntered out while Tree rose to give Marcello an uneasy embrace. Todd was right, the boy had grown since he last saw him. But not too much and certainly not so that anyone would mistake him for an adult. And he had put on some weight. But not much weight. He still retained the round face of an angel. A devilish angel, certainly, but an angel, nonetheless. Not knowing quite what to say, Tree fell back on the universal question asked by all adults unexpectedly encountering children who make them nervous: "How's school going?"

"It's what they call a Teacher In-Service day," Marcello said. "It means they go to school, but we don't."

The boy eased himself into the chair recently vacated by Todd. Tree regained his seat behind the desk. Marcello looked around the room with that combination of child-like innocence and disconcerting worldly awareness Tree remembered from their initial encounter. Marcello was his first client; the boy had a grand total of seven dollars to spend on a private detective. Marcello's father, the nasty Reno O'Hara, willing to sell his son's liver to the highest bidder, had ended up dead, as had his mother, leaving Marcello an orphan in the care of foster parents. Tree had promised to keep in touch with the kid who helped launch whatever his private detective business had amounted to.

And he had kept in touch. Sort of. From time to time.

"How's your family?" Tree asked.

"They aren't my family, but they're okay," Marcello said, referring to the Lakes, the couple he was living with. They had moved onto the island the previous year, and Marcello was now attending the Sanibel School, the island's highly respected middle school on San-Cap Road. Marcello was doing pretty well in the seventh grade. Tree knew that much about the boy's progress.

"So everything's all right?"

"What? You think I only turn up here when things aren't okay? You think maybe I'm here to hire you again?"

"No, of course not," Tree hastened to reassure the boy. "I'm concerned about you, that's all."

"No need to be concerned about me," Marcello said. "In fact, the reason I'm here is because I want to talk to you about what I would call a business proposition."

"A business proposition?" Tree wondered what kind of business proposition a thirteen-year-old boy might be offering. But where Marcello was concerned, anything was possible.

"Yeah, because I know things aren't going so well for you, and I want to maybe help you out."

"What makes you think things aren't going well?"

Marcello looked around the room. "Clients aren't exactly lined up down the stairs, know what I mean?"

Tree smiled and said, "So how are you going to help me, Marcello?"

"Okay, I've started up a new business."

"Have you? What kind of business?"

"The private detecting business."

Tree raised his eyebrows in surprise and said, "Oh?"

Marcello nodded. "I was sort of inspired by you, know what I mean? This whole Sanibel Sunset Detective thing? I figure if grownups needed a detective to find out things for them, kids do, too."

"I see," Tree managed to say. "What are you calling your business?"

"It's called The Sanibel Sunset Detective Agency."

Tree paused to take this in before saying, "Interesting choice of names."

"What I think we should do," Marcello continued, "is form what they call a partnership. You and me together— the two Sanibel Sunset detectives, you might say."

"You might say," Tree said.

"Just to show you I'm bringing something to this, I've got two clients I'm ready to share with you."

"That's very generous," Tree said. "Exactly who are these clients?"

"That's the thing," Marcello said. "I don't want to divulge what you might call their identities until I know we got a deal—for our partnership."

Tree didn't know quite how to respond, so he said, "I'm not sure what to say, Marcello."

"You're blown away by my generosity, I guess."

"That's one way of looking at it," Tree said.

"All you have to do is say, yes."

"Why don't I say, Let me think about it."

Marcello looked surprised. "What's there to think about?"

"For one thing, I'm not so sure it's a good idea to be going into business with a thirteen-year-old. I'm not even sure I can do that."

"Why can't you?"

"To be a private detective—to start your own agency—you have to be licensed by the State of Florida. You're too young, at least for now, to get a license."

"It would be a silent partnership." Marcello said it so fast Tree was certain he had already anticipated this argument and formulated an answer.

"I'd rather you concentrated on your schoolwork." That sounded lame even to Tree.

Marcello wasn't fooled for an instant. "That's adult talk for blow it out your ear."

"I am an adult," Tree said.

"I already told these two clients that I could get them hooked up with you."

"You shouldn't have done that until you talked to me."

"I just talked to you. Can I bring them in?"

"You won't tell me who they are?"

"Not until you meet them."

Tree sighed. "Marcello I'm not comfortable with this."

"Hey, I was your first client." Marcello becoming thirteen-year-old-tough. "You wouldn't even be in business if it wasn't for me."

He had a point there. "Okay, okay," Tree said. "I will talk to these clients of yours. But I doubt there's much I can do to help. When will you bring them?"

"Tomorrow," Marcello said.

"Haven't you got school?"

"We'll come over after school," he said.

"But this doesn't mean we're partners."

Marcello gave him a sweet, innocent smile, as he rose to his feet, a smile that made him look like the guileless kid he most definitely wasn't. "See, you tomorrow," he said.

4

Freddie was in Chicago meeting with the investors group she headed that had acquired the five Dayton's supermarkets in the South Florida area. Thus their house on Captiva Island's Andy Rosse Lane was dark and empty when Tree arrived home that evening with the pre-cooked rotisserie chicken he had acquired at Dayton's.

Tree turned on the lights and placed the chicken on the counter, got himself a Diet Coke from the refrigerator and then sat out by the pool, enjoying the comparative quiet of a Captiva evening—comparative if you discounted the occasional hoot from the merry makers down the street at the Mucky Duck as they celebrated a perfect Florida sunset.

Already he missed Freddie, even though she'd only been gone a day. He missed the glow of her conversation, the warmth of her presence, the quiet, comforting knowledge that two equaled one. This was the way it had been for over ten years, and would continue to be for—a lifetime? Yes, definitely, as far as he was concerned. He could not imagine a life without Fredericka Stayner. But he sometimes wondered about her as he had wondered—as only an ex-newspaperman married four times could wonder—about all the women in his life who had eventually drifted off. In some cases, they had not so much drifted as raced for the nearest exit.

Certainly Freddie was not happy with this new landscape her husband inhabited, this world of the private detective that had turned out to be so much more—what? Complicated? Dangerous? Deceptive? All of the above?

Yes, definitely all of the above.

Particularly the deceptive part. He had become something of a master of deception. Or, as a realist might say in plainer English, a liar. Master of deception sounded much better, of course, as though that required an expertise of sorts. Being a plain, old-fashioned liar didn't require much of anything.

His cellphone sounded. He fished it from his pocket. Speak of the devil: Freddie. "I was just thinking about you," he said into his phone.

"How are you, my love?" Freddie's voice, crackling from Chicago.

"Missing you," he said, with more vehemence than he intended.

She paused a beat before she said, "Is everything okay?"

He considered telling her about his encounter with Owen Markfield that morning, but decided against it. Another strategic omission—or was that also part of the web of lies he tended to spin these days? Whatever it was, he didn't want to worry her or distract her from the business in Chicago, so he merely said, truthfully enough, "Just feeling a little lonely this evening, that's all."

"Well, if it's any consolation, I'm sitting here in my room at the Palmer House feeling the same way," Freddie said.

"No dinner plans?"

"They wanted to go out, but I decided to have something in the room and talk to you instead."

"How did it go today?"

"Well enough, I think," Freddie said. "Everyone seems satisfied with the progress we're making, although we're behind schedule with this new SAP system. Part of the reason I'm here is to see if I can get everyone moving a little faster. What about you? How's business?"

Not good, but he wasn't sure Freddie would want to hear that—or maybe that's exactly what she wanted to hear. He said, "I received a business proposition today."

"Oh? From whom?"

"Marcello O'Hara."

"Our Marcello?"

"The one and only."

"Thirteen-year-old Marcello."

"He wants to go into business with me."

"Doing what?"

"The two Sanibel Sunset detectives. He says he's got a couple of clients for me."

"You're not taking any of this seriously, are you?" A note of concern had worked itself into Freddie's voice.

"No. However, Marcello is bringing his clients around tomorrow."

"Tree, you shouldn't be leading him on."

"I told him we couldn't be partners," Tree said.

"That doesn't sound very definitive."

"Come on, Freddie. He's only thirteen years old. No way can he be my partner."

"How is he, otherwise?"

"He seems fine. Very businesslike. Very Marcello. Focused on one thing. Not very interested in hearing about or discussing anything else."

"But you're not going to do it, are you? You're not going to partner with him."

"I just told you," he said. "What? You think I'm crazy?"

"I'm not going to answer that question," she said good-humoredly. She did say it good-humoredly, didn't she?

"And I haven't even told you about the Oscar show," he said.

"What Oscar show is that?"

"The film society at Big Arts does an annual spoof of the Academy Awards. This year they talked Rex into being master of ceremonies."

"I'll bet they didn't have to do much talking," Freddie said.

"Rex has got me involved. We had our first rehearsal this morning."

"How did it go?"

"I think I'm going to knock 'em dead," Tree said only half-jokingly. "You know when I was younger, before I got into the newspaper business, I thought about becoming an actor."

"There are those who would say you are too good an actor," she said.

"Would you be one of those?"

"What do you think?"

"I would say this is a conversation moving onto dangerous ground," he answered.

They finished with a flurry of "I miss yous" and "I love yous" that were true enough, but left Tree feeling slightly uneasy by the time he hung up. Could Freddie see right through him? Was he in fact a lousy actor when it came to putting anything past her? Probably he was, but a couple of thousand miles away in Chicago she wasn't about to press the point too much. If he wanted to avoid telling her certain things, then she would be patient and save that confrontation for another day.

He was about to go inside to his pre-cooked rotisserie chicken when he heard the scream.

It sounded as though it came from the direction of the Mucky Duck. It was not one of the enthusiastic whoops he usually heard coming from the pub.

This was a genuine, hair-raising scream.

Tree went out onto Andy Rosse Lane just as a police cruiser shot past, siren screaming. Tourists on bikes and strolling along the roadside gaped. Tree saw the cruiser slam to a stop at the end of the road abutting the beach. He jumped back as a second police cruiser whizzed past, and then a third. This was followed by an EMS vehicle, sirens going full blast.

Tree joined other passersby hurrying toward the beach, anxious to discover what was going on. By the time he reached the end of the road, the crowd had grown thick around the cruiser and an EMS van, everyone craning forward, speaking in whispers. The patrons at tables outside the Mucky Duck were out of their seats, some standing on chairs, in order to get a better view.

Behind him, Tree heard more police cars arriving. He pressed through the crowd until he found himself against one of the palm trees that marked the line where the street stopped and the stretch of sandy beach began.

Beyond the palms, Tree could see Detective Owen Markfield walking toward the rolling surf. The sea glinted in tones of black and silver. The sky above was purple and ominous. What looked like a gray, waterlogged sack lay at the water's edge.

It was a moment before Tree realized that the waterlogged sack was in fact a body.

5

Because Freddie wasn't there with an alarm that woke them both on the dot of six a.m., Tree slept in to almost seven. He padded into the kitchen and made himself coffee. There wasn't much about the body on the radio news—a male, in his forties, not yet identified by police. They weren't saying whether foul play was suspected.

Tree sipped his coffee, listened to the radio some more—traffic was heavy along McGregor Boulevard; there was only a ten per cent chance of precipitation today; in addition to the body found on Captiva, unusual, a man had been shot to death in Fort Myers, not unusual. Tree finished his coffee, showered, dressed, and then headed into the office.

As he did each morning, Tree drove past the Traven mansion, and each morning he kept his eyes averted so that he did not have to see the place and did not have to think about what had gone on behind those iron gates, inside those gray stone walls.

Elizabeth Traven, the mansion's beautiful, duplicitous, murderous inhabitant, was still too fresh—and too painful—a memory; a memory he would deny to anyone who asked him about her, particularly Freddie, who always suspected he was infatuated with the late Mrs. Traven. Infatuated or merely intrigued? Another question he chose not to answer, perhaps because he wasn't sure himself. Better just to keep his eyes away and drive past the place—and forget.

But not this morning.

For weeks now there had been activity at the house, trucks arriving and departing. So this morning, on a whim, he pulled the Beetle through the open gates. His progress was blocked by an eighteen-ton dump truck, its hydraulics lifting up the truck bed to spill a load of quarry stone. Immediately, a John Deere skid steer moved forward, the operator lowering the steer's bucket to pick up the stone.

A man in a yellow hard hat, stripped to the waist and wearing dark glasses, appeared at the passenger side window. He leaned down and presented Tree with the blast furnace grin that could only belong to Ryde Bodie.

Ryde said, "Park your car, Tree, and come have a look around."

Surprised—and a little embarrassed to be caught snooping—Tree nodded and pulled the Beetle forward until he found a parking spot beside a contractor's white van. When he got out, Ryde was right there to offer one of his manly handshakes along with a megawatt smile. Ryde's torso was tanned and gleaming with sweat.

"How are you, Tree? Out doing a little private detecting first thing this morning?"

"I was just passing by and thought I'd drop in," Tree said. "I had no idea this was your place."

"I'm probably out of my mind," Ryde said. "But I couldn't resist it. Like the house had my name on it or something. Come on, I'll take you inside." He turned to one of the workers and called, "Charlie, you got a hard hat for my friend?"

Charlie quickly found Tree a hard hat, and handed it to him. Tree put it on and then followed Ryde up the steps to the entrance. Tree said, "Did you hear about the body?"

"What body?" Ryde said.

"A body washed up on the beach last night outside the Mucky Duck," Tree said.

"You don't say? Is that near where you live?"

"Just down the street."

"Another case for Tree Callister," Ryde said.

The familiar stone Great Danes that had glared so many warnings at him during the Traven days remained in place. If only he had listened to those stone dogs, Tree mused. The trouble he could have saved himself.

The entrance doors were open. Ryde removed his sunglasses, stood back to allow a couple of workmen to pass, and then ducked inside, motioning for Tree to follow.

To Tree's amazement, the interior had been gutted so that now it was a vast, open space reverberating with the sound of construction jack hammers, cast in a chalky mist intersected by shafts of sunlight pouring in from the floor-to-ceiling windows overlooking a wide lawn rolling off to the sea.

"We've taken it pretty much right down to the walls," Ryde shouted over the din.

"Why don't you just tear it down and start over?" Tree shouted back.

Ryde shrugged. "There are things about the place I like. Besides, it's a little less expensive to do it this way. Not much, but a little."

They wandered through the rooms, Tree marveling at how any sign of the previous owners had been so thoroughly stripped away.

Once they were outside again, Ryde removed his hard hat, blinked in the sunlight before replacing his sunglasses, and said, "So what do you think, Tree?"

"Well, it's going to be something," was all he could think to say.

"I've got big plans for this place, I do. I'm settling on this island, Tree, and I intend to make it my home. It's paradise here, my shelter from the storm, so to speak. A great place to raise kids."

They were interrupted by the arrival of a heavyset man with inky black hair. He had a thick mustache as black as his hair. He wore a loose-fitting navy shirt over white linen slacks.

Ryde said, "Excuse me a minute will you, Tree?"

He walked over to the man saying, "Hey, Diego."

Over the construction sounds, Tree could not make out what they were saying, but it sounded like Ryde was speaking Spanish to the black-haired man he had called Diego. The black-haired man shook his head and said angrily in English loud enough for Tree to hear: "To hell with you, man. Why didn't you call me, like you said?"

Ryde, looking unperturbed, spoke again in Spanish. The black-haired man replied in a raised voice but this time he, too, spoke Spanish.

This back-and-forth in Spanish continued for several minutes. Finally, the black-haired man abruptly smacked his hand against Ryde's chest, knocking him back. Tree went over to the two men and said, "Everything all right?"

The black-haired man called Diego turned with lazy nonchalance to Tree, eyeing him as if measuring him for a coffin. "Who are you, hombre?" he said in English.

Ryde had regained his composure and now stepped forward. "It's okay, Tree. Diego and I are old friends."

Diego looked at Ryde in a way that suggested many things, none of them friendship.

Ryde added in a hopeful voice, "Diego sometimes loses his temper, but that's all it is, right Diego?"

The black-haired man didn't answer, but continued to focus on Tree. "Who is your friend?" he said, addressing Ryde.

"Tree's all right, he's fine," Ryde said.

"He should learn to mind his business," Diego said.

"Listen, I'm going to walk Tree back to his car, Diego. Why don't you wait here and then we can finish our conversation."

"No, that's okay," Diego said, finally dragging his eyes away from Tree. "You and me, we can talk later." He looked around at the dust-clogged space, the trucks and vans, the workmen moving back and forth. "Nice place," he said. "Big man with a lot of money has a place like this."

He delivered one last hot-eyed glare at Tree and Ryde before turning on his heel and walking away.

"Your friend's not very happy," Tree said.

"Diego's okay," Ryde said. "We're involved in a couple of business things. He's a bit of a hothead, gets a little impatient."

"That's the business of bringing people together?" Tree said.

Ryde grinned and said, "That's all it is, Tree. Bringing people together for mutual benefit."

He draped his arm across Tree's shoulders, old pals. "Tell you what, Tree, I might be in need of the services of a private investigator like yourself in the next little while."

"To protect you from guys like Diego?"

Ryde looked at him for a long beat before he said, "I don't think you'd be much use to me where Diego is concerned." Then he smiled and slapped Tree's arm. "I've got your card. How be I give you a call?"

"Sure, Ryde," Tree said. "Why don't you do that?" Tree remembered to remove his hard hat. He could not imagine how goofy he looked wearing it. "You'd better take this," he said, handing the hat to Ryde.

"It's great to see you Tree," he said. "Thanks for stopping by."

Tree started into his car, feeling as he always felt when visiting the Traven mansion—uneasy. He turned to look at the stone dogs peering down at him through the mist of dust thrown off by the workmen tearing away at the house. Their eyes were, as always, blank yet somehow full of warning.

6

Marcello was already in the office by the time Tree arrived. "You're like gonna have to get here earlier if we're partners," Marcello said. He didn't sound as though he was kidding.

"I'll try to keep that in mind," Tree said, seating himself at his desk. "I thought you were coming after school."

"My clients would rather do it during their lunch hour," Marcello said.

"Where are they?"

"They'll be here in a few minutes," Marcello said. "In the meantime, we should talk about what they call the financial arrangements."

"What financial arrangements?"

"For our partnership."

"Marcello," Tree said, "there is no partnership."

"I would say we split things fifty-fifty," Marcello said.

"You would, would you?"

"Unless you got a better idea."

"My idea is that right now you should concentrate on school work and not worry about being a private detective. I can take care of that end of things just fine."

"No offense, but from what I can see, you could use some help," Marcello said.

"Well, that's your opinion," Tree said.

"Isn't just my opinion." Marcello rose in his chair to peer out the window behind Tree. "Here they are now."

Tree swiveled around in time to see a Lincoln Town Car pull into the parking lot and come to a stop. A young man with a shaved head, wearing a dark suit, emerged from the car and held open the passenger door. A moment or so later, a boy and a girl clambered out and disappeared into the Visitors Center.

Tree turned back to Marcello. "Those are your clients?"

Marcello gave him a look of satisfaction. "Told you they'd be here."

"Marcello, what's going on?"

"What do you mean?"

"Your clients arrive in a chauffeured town car?"

Marcello grinned.

The boy and girl climbed the stairs and appeared at the door. The boy was about twelve years old, with sandy hair, neatly dressed in gray linen pants topped by a crimson Ralph Lauren Polo shirt. The girl was a year or so younger, a budding blond beauty in a white top and pink shorts. They both wore smart-looking backpacks and looked like models in an ad for expensive children's clothing, solemn-faced as they shook Tree's hand and Marcello made introductions.

"This is Madison and Joshua," he said in a formal voice. "Madison and Joshua, I want you to meet Tree Callister, the very important private detective I was telling you about."

The boy Joshua said in a somber voice, "Who's your favorite WWE wrestler?"

"I told you not to ask that question," Madison snapped.

"I'm just asking," defended Joshua.

"It's a stupid question," Madison pronounced.

"I'm not certain I have a favorite wrestler," Tree said.

"Mine is Rey Mysterio," Joshua said.

The little girl, Madison, addressed Tree in a business-like voice. "Mr. Callister, do you mind if I speak frankly?"

"Not at all," Tree said.

Madison said, "You seem a little old to be a private detective."

"I told you about that," interjected Marcello. "I said he looked old but he can still do what he has to do."

Joshua glared at his sister. "Madison, you shouldn't talk like that. It's rude."

"I'm just saying," Madison replied. "We should talk about these things, shouldn't we?"

Tree raised his voice to say, "Why don't you all tell me why you are here. After that, we can decide whether I'm too old or not."

Madison looked at Joshua. "Go ahead. You tell him."

Joshua shook his head. "No, you tell it. It's your idea."

"My idea?" Madison seemed appalled at the suggestion. "It was not *my* idea I can tell you that much."

"I'm saying it's your idea, stupid," Joshua hissed, "because we are not supposed to say *whose* idea it was."

"Then say it's *your* idea."

Tree looked at Marcello, who shrugged and said, "They're worried about their father."

"That's right," Joshua piped up, suddenly enthusiastic, not wanting Marcello to steal the spotlight. "We *are* worried."

"*Concerned*," amended Madison. "The correct word is *concerned*."

"Concerned, worried, they're the same thing," Joshua said.

"No, they are not." Madison, adamant. "Worried is, like, we're not sleeping at night. Concerned is, you know, we're a *little* worried."

"What are you worried about?" Tree, attempting to get the conversation back on track.

"We are *concerned* that ever since he moved here, Father has been acting strangely," Joshua said.

"Where are you from?" Tree asked.

"We lived in Charlotte," Joshua said.

"We liked it there, but we don't like it here so much," Madison added.

"Why not?" Tree asked.

"That's when the weird stuff started happening," Joshua said.

"Father began going out at night and not coming back until almost dawn," Madison asserted.

"He didn't do that in Charlotte?" Tree asked.

"I don't think so," Joshua said.

"He thinks we're asleep," added Madison.

"We have no idea where he goes," said Joshua.

"Have you asked him? Maybe there is a reasonable explanation."

"Then there are the phone calls," Joshua said.

Madison: "People phone and when we answer, they hang up."

"Also," Joshua said, "people are watching the house."

"Watching the house? Are you sure about that?"

Joshua and Madison traded glances. "Yes," Madison said with a decisive nod. "It's creepy."

"Very creepy," Joshua emphasized.

Tree asked, "What does your father do for a living?"

Once again Madison and Joshua shot glances back and forth. "We don't know," Madison said.

"That's the trouble," Joshua said. "We don't."

"But we suspect," Madison said.

"I wouldn't exactly say we suspect," Joshua said. "It's more like we are worried."

"*Concerned*," Madison amended.

"About what?" Tree demanded.

"That he's involved in some sort of . . . *criminal enterprise.*"

The words seemed to hang ominously in the air, bringing silence to the room.

Tree broke that silence when he said, "What would you like me to do?"

The two children looked at him in disbelief. "We want you to find out, of course," Madison said.

"Find out what?"

Madison said, "Find out what he's up to."

"After all," Joshua added, "this is Florida. Who knows what goes on?"

"Marcello says the two of you are partners," Madison said. "He said you would help us."

"First of all, Marcello and I aren't partners," Tree said.

Madison shot Marcello a dirty look. Marcello shrugged and said, "We're in what they call a negotiation."

"Look," Tree said, "I understand the concern you have about your father. I used to wonder what my father did when I was a kid. However, I discovered the best way to find out was not by hiring a private detective."

"What was that?" Madison trained pale blue eyes directly at Tree. "What was the best way?"

"I asked him," Tree said.

Madison said: "We tried that."

"What did he say?"

"He didn't say anything," Madison said.

"What about your mother? What's she have to say about all this?"

There was a long pause before Joshua said, "We don't have a mother."

"She's dead," pronounced Madison, ever the realist.

"I'm sorry," Tree said.

Marcello said, "There is no doubt this dude is up to something, and my friends here are worried."

"*Concerned*," Madison once again interjected.

"I think we can help them, don't you?" Marcello the problem-solver.

"We have money." Joshua said this in a way that suggested that was the clincher.

"There you go," Marcello said.

"We might be able to come up with as much as twenty-five dollars," Joshua declared.

"*If* we get the results we're looking for," added Madison.

"Fifty per cent of that would be yours," Marcello said to Tree.

Tree tried not to smile. "I'm coming up in the world, Marcello. The last time you hired me, I only earned seven dollars." He focused on Madison and Joshua. "However, I don't think employing me to investigate your father is the answer you're looking for."

"Why not?" said Madison. "Adults use detectives all the time to find out things about their wives and their husbands, even their kids. Why can't kids hire someone to find out about their father?"

"I just don't think I'm the person for this," Tree said.

To Tree's amazement, Joshua's eyes welled with tears. "Something is wrong," he said in a quivering voice.

Madison sounded equally frantic. "They're going to *hurt* our father, I just know it."

"Who do you think is going to hurt him?" Tree asked.

Madison stared at him, starting to tremble, tears in her eyes, too.

"Please don't cry," Tree said.

"I'm *not* crying," Madison blubbered. "I *don't* cry!"

"Marcello said you would help us," chimed in Joshua, his voice breaking with emotion.

Tree sat there, not knowing quite what to say.

"There's no one else to go to," Madison said.

Joshua's stricken, tear-stained face, Marcello's anxious look, and Madison's imploring, teary glare. Damn, he thought to himself. How did he manage to get himself into these messes?

He looked at Madison and said, "What's your father's name?"

"Granger," Madison said instantly. "Wayne Granger." She sat up straight in her chair. The tears had magically disappeared.

"Do you have a photograph of him?"

"That's the other thing," Joshua said. "He won't let anyone take his picture."

"Who drove you over here this morning?"

"That's our driver," Joshua said. His tears were gone, too. "His name is Curtis."

"You have a driver named Curtis?"

"That's right," Joshua said.

"Did you tell him why you are here?"

"No," Madison said. "We told Curtis that we were coming to the Visitors Center for a school project."

"That was my idea," said Marcello.

"We told him that," Joshua added, "because he tells our father everything. He's sort of Dad's spy."

"And he scares us," Madison said. "We don't think he's up to much good, either."

"Okay, where do you live?"

"Right now, we're on Rabbit Road."

"What's the number?"

"Five fifty-five," said Joshua.

"My wife's right," Tree said. The three kids looked at him. "She thinks I'm crazy."

The kids gazed at him as if crazy was the most natural thing in the world.

"All right, let me see what I can do."

Relieved expressions flooded the three apprehensive faces aligned before him. "But I'm not promising anything, okay?"

Madison stood and unslung her backpack. Then she extracted a pink-laminated wallet, opened it up and carefully withdrew a couple of wrinkled ten dollar bills and put them on the desk in front of Tree. "We're going to have to owe you the rest," she said.

"It's all right," Tree said. "Let's see what I can do before we start worrying about how I'm going to get paid."

"No, no," Marcello said, grabbing for the bills. "We'll take the money."

"Marcello," Tree said with a warning tone in his voice.

Marcello sighed and handed the bills back to Madison. "This is no way to start a partnership, working for free," he said in a sullen voice.

"We are not partners," Tree said.

Marcello did not look convinced.

7

B last Marcello, anyway, Tree thought as he huddled inside the Beetle, tired, thirsty—why did he always forget to bring bottled water on these stakeouts?—and now his sciatic nerve was acting up, sending sharp pulses of pain down his leg. How did he get talked into these things? What was he doing with what little life he had left in him cramped into a tiny car in the night hoping to get a glimpse of—what? He wasn't even sure of *that*.

As soon as the kids left his office, he had Googled Wayne Granger's name. Wayne Granger was a former major league baseball right-handed relief pitcher who had played for teams that included the St. Louis Cardinals. Tree doubted he was the kids' dad. Another Wayne Granger sold real estate in Washington, Pennsylvania. There was also a Wayne Granger who lived outside Montreal, Quebec. But there was no Wayne Granger living on the west coast of Florida, at least not one who came up in the search engine.

So who was the Wayne Granger at number five fifty-five Rabbit Road?

The house stood at the end of a laneway. There was a For Lease sign beside the mail box. When Tree arrived, he had parked down the way and then walked back to the mail box. Through the palm trees forming a barrier along the road he could see a frame structure on stilts with a screened-in porch. A light from the house shone through the trees. Otherwise, the inky blackness of the night pressed in on him. Huddled in the repositioned Beetle, he felt exposed. If someone came along asking questions what possible excuse could he have for being parked at the side of a residential street?

The cellphone on the seat beside him started vibrating. He picked it up and saw that it was Freddie.

"Hi, my darling," he said into the phone.

"What are you up to?" Freddie said.

"I'm sitting here counting the number of ways I've misspent my life," he said.

"Well, you're not doing it at home. Where are you?"

"Outside some guy's house on Rabbit Road."

"Dare I ask why?"

"I wish you wouldn't."

"Let me put it this way," Freddie said. "Is it dangerous?"

"It's worse than dangerous," Tree said. "It's boring."

"Personally, my love, I opt for boring over dangerous. Do you have a new client?"

"I'm not sure. Sort of, I suppose."

"What does that mean?"

"It means that Marcello has once again talked me into something I should never have been talked into."

"Tree, for heaven's sake. I thought you weren't going to do this."

"His two clients, kids, showed up in a chauffeured Lincoln worried about their father."

"A chauffeur drove them to your office?"

"His name is Curtis."

"What do they want you to do?"

"They want me to find out what their father is up to."

"And that's why you're sitting outside a house on Rabbit Road in the middle of the night?"

"Correct."

There was a long pause before Freddie said, "So now you're partners with Marcello?"

"The two Sanibel Sunset detectives." Tree said it with a certain amount of ruefulness in his voice.

"Tree, tell me that's not going to happen."

"No, of course not."

"Except it already has happened."

"I got talked into doing this one thing, that's all," Tree said. "And I'm sitting here kicking myself for it."

There was another long pause, followed by a sigh, before Freddie said, "I hope you know what you're doing."

"As usual, I don't think I do."

"Please, please, Tree, stay out of trouble."

"I don't think there's much trouble here, just boredom," Tree said.

He no sooner uttered the words than a bright light flooded the Beetle. He squinted into the rear view mirror and saw a car pull up behind him. He said to Freddie, "I've got to go."

"Everything okay?"

"Everything's fine," Tree said. "I'll call you later."

He placed his phone on the seat beside him. In the side view mirror he could see someone leave the car. Tree opened the driver's door and eased out. He straightened as Detective Owen Markfield came toward him.

"Well, well," Markfield said. "Imagine finding Sanibel's intrepid private detective out here in the darkness on Rabbit Road."

Tree didn't say anything. Markfield had a flashlight which he now shone on Tree. "Are you armed?" he said.

"No," Tree answered.

"Tell you what, Tree. Why don't you come back toward my car, turn around, and place your hands on the hood."

"Come on, Markfield. You know I don't have a gun."

Markfield's voice tightened when he said, "Don't make me ask you again."

Tree exhaled loudly and then moved back to Markfield's car and spread his arms out and positioned his hands against the hood. He felt Markfield pat him down. "Okay, Tree, you can turn around now."

Tree turned and Markfield shone the light into his eyes. "You want to tell me what you're doing here?"

"Just out for a drive," was all Tree could think of to say.

"It's almost midnight."

"I couldn't sleep," Tree said. "Is it against the law to drive around Sanibel Island at night?"

"You weren't driving, Tree. You're parked on the side of the road. Also, we had a call reporting a suspicious person in the area."

"So you just happened to be on duty, is that it, Detective?"

"I want you to turn around, Tree," Markfield said.

"Why do you want me to do that?"

Markfield took a step forward, balled his fist, and jabbed it into Tree's stomach. He collapsed to the ground, choking for air.

"You've got to learn not to ask so many questions," he dimly heard Markfield say.

Then Tree heard another voice: "What's going on here?"

A figure appeared—Ryde Bodie in shorts and a T-shirt, carrying a flashlight.

Markfield stared at the newcomer. Ryde helped Tree to his feet. "You okay, Tree?"

Markfield said, "Who are you?"

"I'm Ryder Bodie. I rent the house down the lane. I heard a commotion and came out. The question is, who are you?"

Markfield opened up the billfold that contained his Sanibel Police identification. Ryde nodded and said, "What brings you out here, Detective?"

"You know this man?" Markfield pointed at Tree.

"Private Detective Tree Callister is doing some work for me," Ryde said in the sort of easy, reassuring voice that somehow made everything seem normal, even threatening cops in the middle of the night.

Markfield looked surprised—and then suspicious. "Yeah? What kind of work is he doing for you?"

"As you know there have been a lot of break-ins recently on the island. I'm renting this place until renovations are completed on my house on Captiva Drive. Meanwhile, I've got two small children, and I want to make certain they're protected. I've hired Mr. Callister to keep an eye on the house at night, report anything suspicious."

Markfield looked at Tree. "What about it, Callister? You see anything suspicious tonight?"

"The only suspicious thing I've seen is what appears to be an assault on one of my employees," Ryde Bodie said.

"I don't know what you're talking about," Markfield said. But in the wash of headlights, Tree caught a flicker of concern.

Ryde, very much in command, casually turned to Tree. "What about it, Tree? Did this man attack you?"

Tree studied Markfield for a couple of long beats before he said, "Detective Markfield was investigating reports of an intruder in the neighborhood. I think he was only trying to serve and protect. Isn't that right, Detective Markfield?"

Markfield's lip curled. "Don't think this changes anything, Callister. We'll meet up another time."

"It's always good to see you, Detective," Tree said, keeping his voice even.

Markfield gave Ryde Bodie a hard look and then wheeled around and walked back to his car.

He got inside, started the engine, and spun onto the roadway, throwing up a spray of dirt and gravel in his wake. The world descended into darkness. Ryde Bodie's arm moved and Tree could see that he was holding something black and ugly.

It took him a moment to realize it was a gun.

Pointed at him.

8

Tree managed to say, "What are you going to do with that?"

"Generally in South Florida guns are used to shoot people," Ryde Bodie said.

"I thought they were for target practice."

"They just say that so you can shoot people," Ryde said.

"How many people have you shot?"

"This is what they call the Fabrique Nationale," Ryde said evenly. "It's more commonly known as the FN Five-seven. It can penetrate a police officer's Kevlar vest. You're damned lucky I didn't shoot you with it."

"Detective Markfield will be sorry to hear he saved my life," Tree said.

"This is not a good time to come creeping around my house in the middle of the night."

"Sorry about that," Tree said.

"I can't see a thing out here." Ryde lowered his gun. "Let's go inside. I could use a drink, and we can talk."

Ryde snapped on his flashlight again, and Tree followed its wavering beam along the laneway to the house. The two men climbed a steep flight of stairs to the screened-in porch and into a sitting room illuminated by a single lamp. The light fell on two ugly brown love seats facing one another.

"Come on," Ryde said. "I want to check on the kids."

He veered down a short corridor and opened the first door on his right. Light from the hall fell across twin beds revealing Madison in pink pajamas sprawled on her back. On the adjacent bed, only the top of what Tree imagined was Joshua's head was visible above the covers.

"They are wonderful," Ryde said. "Especially when they are sound asleep." He threw a telling glance at Tree. "And not sneaking around, hiring private detectives."

Tree tried not to look embarrassed—and failed miserably. "How did you find out?"

"Your young clients were so proud of themselves, they couldn't keep quiet about it. I only had to reprimand Madison once before she was warning me that she and Joshua had hired a detective who would soon make me pay for my many transgressions."

Tree rolled his eyes, and said, "Oh, no."

Ryde grinned and said, "Let's get that drink I talked about."

When they came back into the sitting room, Curtis, the big chauffeur who had driven the children that morning, was waiting in the kitchen holding a semi-automatic weapon. He held it in a way that suggested he knew how to use it.

"Did you meet Curtis?" Ryde asked.

Tree nodded. "I didn't recognize him with the gun in his hand."

"That's an AR15 Assault Rifle," Ryde said.

"Of course," Tree said. "Who in South Florida doesn't have one?"

Ryde laughed and said, "Curtis drives the kids, and helps with security."

Tree looked at him and said, "You need a guy with an assault rifle for security?"

Ryde said, "What would you like to drink?"

"I'm okay, thanks."

Ryde's eyebrows shot up and down. "You don't drink?"

"Not anymore," Tree said.

"I need a scotch after all this." He nodded to Curtis. "Do me a favor, Curtis, check around outside, make sure we don't have any more visitors."

Curtis nodded and went out through the porch. Tree heard the sound of his heavy footsteps going down the stairs.

Ryde disappeared into the kitchen and came back a couple of minutes later holding a tumbler three-quarters full of amber-colored liquid. "Sit down, will you?" He indicated one of the sofas. "Sure I can't get you something?"

"No thanks," Tree said.

Ryde settled onto a sofa and shook his head. "A detective who doesn't drink, who takes on ten-year-old clients, and has the Sanibel Island cops breathing down his neck. An interesting combination."

"I may not be much of a detective, but I do know worried kids when I see them—and Joshua and Madison certainly are concerned about you."

"Their mother was killed in a car accident three years ago," Ryde said quietly.

"I'm sorry, I didn't know."

"I was driving at the time. Joshua and Madison hold me responsible for what happened, and I can't say as I blame them. But the fact is, since then, they've concocted all sorts of wild ideas about me. We've all been through a tough time. I try to keep that in mind when I'm dealing with my children."

"I'm sorry if I've complicated things for you," Tree said.

"Well, now you know something about my background, Tree."

When in fact Tree didn't know much of anything.

Ryde continued: "How about you? What are you? A former police officer?"

"No," Tree said. "I was a reporter in Chicago. For the *Sun-Times*. I was downsized a couple of years ago. My wife and I decided to move to Sanibel Island so she could take a job at Dayton's."

"Now she owns the store?"

"She doesn't put it quite that way," Tree said.

"She's done well for herself." And Tree hadn't? Is that what he was getting at?

Ryde swallowed some of his scotch. "Tell me, what you did to rile up that cop?"

"He doesn't like me." Tree saw no point in getting into the real reason behind Markfield's hostility.

Ryde again raised and lowered his eyebrows. "And here you seem like such a likable guy."

"Look, I'm sorry about all this," Tree said. "The kids came in today with a young fellow I've been close to. I didn't have the heart to say no to him—or to them."

"You must have been at least somewhat intrigued," Ryde said. "What did they tell you, anyway?"

"They didn't tell me much of anything," Tree said. "It's not what they know about their father. It's what they don't know. They wanted me to find out what they don't know about someone who turns out to be you—although the kids gave me another name."

Ryde drank more scotch before he said, "Did they?"

"They said you were Wayne Granger."

If this surprised or upset Ryde, he didn't show it. But then Tree was beginning to suspect Ryder Bodie excelled when it came to the business of hiding emotions. He finished the scotch.

"It's probably a good thing I encountered you tonight."

Tree couldn't help but sound surprised when he said, "It is?"

Ryde put his glass down and leaned back against the cushions of the sofa. "I'm leaving town for a couple of weeks, and I'm taking the children with me. I could use someone to watch the house. Would you do something like that? I'd need you to basically do what you've done tonight. Drive around regularly, check this house and the one on Captiva Drive, make sure everything's okay."

Tree was about to say that checking on houses wasn't exactly in his wheel house. But then children could hire him for twenty-five dollars so he decided to keep his mouth shut and, for the moment at least, go along with Ryde Bodie who was also Wayne Granger.

"What about it, Tree? Are you up for it? You can charge me whatever your rate is. I can write you a check now."

"It's all right," Tree said. "We can settle up later—but I'll need your real name."

"Why would you need that?"

"They taught us that at detective school," Tree said. "Make sure you get a client's real name."

"The kids know me as Wayne Granger. For business reasons, I'm Ryder Bodie."

"So I should call you Ryde."

"Sure," Ryde said with a wave of his hand. "Call me anything you want."

Tree said, "When are you leaving?"

"Later today. I'll be gone a couple of weeks. You'd be doing me a great favor."

Would he? Out loud, Tree said, "Okay."

"See, Tree? This evening has worked out great for both of us."

Ryde was on his feet, grinning—that megawatt Ryder Bodie grin Tree was getting all too accustomed to.

Ryde Bodie who was Wayne Granger.

9

At three o'clock in the morning, without Freddie beside him, Tree couldn't sleep. He got out of bed, padded across the bedroom and opened the door into what appeared to be an airplane hangar. Catwalks crisscrossed the upper reaches of the structure where big Klieg-type lights hung. Out on the concrete floor, someone was driving a golf cart in circles.

When the young man at the wheel spotted Tree, he drove the golf cart over. The young man wore the dress khakis of a U.S. Army sergeant. A round baby face was framed with jet-black hair, short at the sides, but swept up into a high pompadour.

"Sir, you don't happen to be a guitar player," the young man said in a pleasant Southern drawl.

"I've always wanted to play the guitar," Tree said.

"Yeah, well, the difference between a guitar player and a guy who wants to play the guitar is that the guitar player can play the guitar."

"I can see that," Tree said.

"We're gonna lay down some tracks tonight, and we could use a good guitar player."

"Sorry," Tree said.

The young man got out of the golf cart and came over to where Tree stood. Tree marveled at the perfect fit of his uniform. It looked as though it had been sewn on him.

"You can't sleep either, huh?"

"My wife's in Chicago," Tree said. "I always have trouble sleeping when she's gone."

"I ain't got no wife, man, I just have trouble sleeping, period. So sometimes I come over here and just drive this golf cart around."

"Are you in the army?" Tree asked.

"Well, I was in the army but not anymore."

"You just can't stop wearing the uniform, is that it?"

The young man laughed and shook his head. "Nah, I'm sort of into this acting thing now, so the part I'm playing, the guy's a G.I. stationed in Germany. We're shooting on the stage next door. I just came over here to get away.

"See, I have this recurring dream that I've lost it all, everything I worked for is gone, and I'm all alone. Man, that dream scares me more than anything, makes me want to get into a golf cart and just drive around in circles till I shake the damn thing off."

Tree said, "What keeps me awake at night is that after a lifetime of work, I've got nothing—that's no dream, it's a reality. I'm not sure how that happened. I got up and went to work every day of my life, and I ended up with nothing."

"There you go, that's exactly what bothers me. It can happen. You can lose everything you've ever worked for. Before you know it, it all just slips away."

"It's not as though I lost all that much when I think about it—I never had very much to begin with. At this time of night, I'm haunted by the mistakes I made. At the moment I made them, they didn't seem like anything, but they add up after a while, and you realize you've paid a pretty high price for your carelessness and your screw-ups."

"That's what I don't want to happen to me," the young man said. "But I'm kind of obsessed with the fear that it will."

"You're an actor?" Tree said.

"That's what they call it," the young man said, "although sometimes I wonder."

"I thought a lot about becoming an actor when I was younger. Maybe I should have gotten into that, instead of journalism. Maybe I'd be better off today."

"I don't know, sir, this acting thing, I'm really not all that comfortable with it. I like singing better."

"I don't know what it is, but lately I just have this feeling I should have pursued it," Tree said. "I have this vision of myself on a horse, tanned and rugged, not saying too much but just having this incredibly strong presence on the screen."

"Take it from me, sir, you may see yourself that way, but the first thing you know, they got you singing to a turtle—and *that* becomes how the world sees you."

"It doesn't make a whole lot of difference at this point," Tree said. "Everything is coming to an end. Most of the people I grew up with, whether they made it or didn't make it, they're gone now, and what they did or didn't do doesn't make a whole lot of difference."

"Don't that beat all?" the young man said with a rueful laugh. "Here we are, a couple of guys hanging out late at night, unable to sleep, scared as hell about life."

A door at the far end of the hangar-like structure opened, and three men appeared. "They're waiting for you on the set, Boss," one of the men called.

The young man delivered a lazy smile. Despite the funny haircut he really is handsome, Tree thought.

"Guess I got to be going," the young man said.

"Take care of yourself," Tree said. The two of them shook hands.

"I'll be seeing you around," the young man said.

"Do you think so?" Tree said.

"You can count on it," said the young man.

He got back in the golf cart and drove to where the three men waited. He stopped the golf cart, and the three men whisked him through the connecting door. Tree was left alone in this vast space. He was very tired suddenly. He really did need to get more sleep. Maybe if he just lay down on the floor for a couple of minutes.

Yes, this wasn't so bad, he thought as he stretched out on his back. He would briefly shut his eyes. A cat nap. Then he would be able to face the world again, a world increasingly difficult to face. From somewhere in the distance, he could hear singing. Unless he missed his guess, the song was "Frankfurt Special" from *G.I. Blues*. Wasn't that curious? he thought as he drifted off. Go special, go. Blow whistle, blow.

What?

Tree jerked awake, alone in bed. It was morning. He sat on the edge of the bed thinking about black-haired young men in golf carts, missing Freddie. He almost picked up the phone so he could tell her how he had been caught red-handed, first by Owen Markfield and then—and this was most embarrassing—by the father of the two children he had been dumb enough to take on as clients; a father who, it turned out, he already knew. The father who had now hired the ignominious detective, although why he would do that in the wake of Tree's stumblebum performance was anyone's guess.

He decided not to phone Freddie. She already thought him mad for having anything to do with the kids in the first place. Discussion of last night's events would only confirm her growing suspicion—albeit a suspicion she diplomatically kept to herself—that in addition to being crazy, her husband was a fool.

Still, when you go by at least two names, employ a bodyguard who carries an assault rifle, and you won't say a whole lot about what you do for a living, you could hardly blame the kids for wondering about their father. Tree wondered himself. Whatever it was, Ryde Bodie wasn't selling insurance for a living.

He got off the bed and went out into the kitchen and started to make coffee. He was interrupted by a knock on the front door. He crossed the living room and opened the door to find Marcello frowning up at him. "It's like nine o'clock in the morning, and you're not dressed or shaved or anything," he said in an accusatory voice.

"What are you doing here?" Tree demanded.

"Checking up on you," Marcello shot back. "Some partner you're turning out to be."

"I'm not your partner, and you should be in school."

"Can I come in or not?"

Tree opened the door wider. "Get in here. Have you had anything to eat?"

"I don't eat breakfast," Marcello said.

"What do you mean you don't eat breakfast? You're a kid. You should eat breakfast."

"You got a banana? I could eat a banana."

Tree marched Marcello into the kitchen and got him a banana. Marcello sat at the table carefully peeling the fruit.

Tree said, "Eat that, and then I'm driving you to school."

Marcello frowned. "I'm worried about Joshua and Madison."

"Listen, I'm in a lot of trouble because of you and those kids."

"They're not answering their cellphones this morning."

"They've got cellphones?"

"Of course. All kids got cellphones."

"Do you have a cellphone?"

"Couldn't survive without one," Marcello said. He took a nibble on his banana, as if testing to ensure Tree hadn't poisoned it.

"I saw Joshua and Madison last night," Tree said. "They're fine."

Marcello looked up from his banana. "What are you talking about? Where did you see them?"

"On Rabbit Road, after their father caught me watching the house."

Marcello frowned. "You weren't supposed to get caught."

"Now you tell me," Tree said irritably. "The point being, their father is not happy that his children are hiring private detectives to spy on him."

"That's because he's dangerous and a crook. Dudes like that don't like to be watched." Marcello made it sound as though he had experience dealing with the likes and dislikes of dangerous dudes.

Tree thought of the guy named Curtis with the assault rifle, and Ryde's FN Five-seven. "Whatever he is, he is not a threat to his children."

"Yeah? Then how come they're not answering their phones?"

"Maybe because they're going away with their father today."

Now it was Marcello's turn to look surprised. "They never told me anything about that."

"Like I said, I talked to their father last night—feeling like a fool, incidentally."

"Why would you feel like that?"

"I suppose because I allowed three children to talk me into sitting outside someone's house in the middle of the night."

"I'm not a child," Marcello protested.

Tree rolled his eyes. "Do you want anything else to eat? If not, I'm driving you over to the school."

Marcello shook his head. "We gotta take care of this problem."

"*We* don't have to take care of anything. *You* have to go to school."

"I tell you this dude is up to no good," Marcello said.

"I'm keeping an eye on his house for him," Tree said.

"You're doing *what?*" Marcello was frowning again.

"Keeping an eye on the Rabbit Road house. The place on Captiva Drive as well. If something is amiss, I'll be able to spot it."

"Something is *amiss* all right," Marcello said. "What's *amiss*, the bad dude has bought you off. You being my partner and everything."

"I'm not your partner, Marcello."

"You sure aren't acting like any partner I'd want to have," he said angrily.

"Come on, I'm driving you over to the school."

Marcello got up from the table, grumbling: "No way to treat a partnership, letting some bad dude buy you off."

"Nobody's bought me off. I wish they would. That way I wouldn't have to put up with this nonsense. How did you get here, anyway?"

"My bike's outside," Marcello said.

"Let's get it and put it in the garage for now. You can get it back later."

"I don't need no ride," Marcello said sullenly.

"Marcello," Tree said in the sort of warning parental voice he had not had to use for a long time.

Marcello groaned and went out the door. Tree followed him. Marcello's red bike was in the drive, chipped and banged up since the last time Tree had seen it. He put it in the garage and then went back out to the Beetle. Marcello waited in the passenger seat.

When they got over to the school, Tree pulled into the drive and stopped the car. For a moment, Marcello didn't move.

"Hey," Tree said. "Are you okay?"

Marcello seemed to take a deep breath and then turned to Tree. "He killed their mom."

"What?"

"That dude who's now hired you, he killed Joshua and Madison's mom."

"Their mother died in a car accident," Tree replied. "Ryde was driving the car. He didn't intentionally kill his wife, Marcello."

"Yeah, well that's what you're saying, because that's what you adults tell each other, and you believe one another. But the kids, man, they got another story. It wasn't no car and it wasn't no accident."

"You're wrong, Marcello."

"How do you know that? Look at this another way, the kids' way. They're afraid of him. They think maybe they're next. This is adult stuff, okay? I can't handle it. That's why I need your help, even though you're not much. Right now, you're all those kids got. You gotta protect them."

Before Tree could say anything, Marcello had opened the passenger door, hopped outside, and was running for the school.

10

Still shaken by what Marcello had told him, Tree drove to his office. The local news on WGCU reported police had still not identified the body found on the beach at Captiva Island. The investigation was continuing.

Marcello seemed to know exactly how to push his buttons: drop an intriguing uncertainty just when he thought he had everything figured out; create doubt as to whether he had done the right thing at the moment he was certain he *had* done the right thing—and then disappear before he had to answer questions.

Clever kid. Too clever. And exasperating to boot.

But supposing Marcello was right? What if Joshua and Madison Ryder were in danger? Supposing their father did kill their mother?

Supposing kids really did see things from a different perspective than adults.

Supposing Ryde Bodie really was the bad dude Marcello accused him of being.

Tree, driving. Thinking.

There was one person who might be able to help him answer some of these questions—or at least put him on the right track. But would Sanibel Island Detective Cee Jay Boone even take his call, let alone help him? Cee Jay and her partner had tried to kill him as he pursued his first case. Cee Jay claimed she had just been trying to scare him. The charges against her had been thrown out on a technicality, forcing the Sanibel Police Department to reinstate her. They had encountered each other several times since and, at the most unlikely moments, Cee Jay had come to his aid. Maybe she would do it again.

"Tree, I can't talk to you," Cee Jay said as soon as she came on the phone.

"Wayne Granger," Tree said.

That drew a long silence on the other end of the line. Tree said, "Cee Jay? Are you there?"

Cee Jay said, "What do you know about him?"

"What do *you* know about him?"

"Why would I know anything?"

"Cee Jay, you know something. I can tell by your voice."

"You can't tell anything from my voice," she insisted.

"Yes, I can. Tell me what you know about him."

"What I know is that you *shouldn't* know that name."

"Why shouldn't I, Cee Jay?"

"All I can tell you is that Wayne Granger is the subject of an ongoing federal investigation, and therefore you should stay as far away as you possibly can."

And then Cee Jay hung up.

Federal investigation? Wayne Granger was the *subject* of a federal investigation? That meant Ryde Bodie was also the subject—Granger and Bodie being one and the same.

What kind of federal investigation would that be? He wondered as he turned into the parking lot at the Chamber of Commerce Visitors Center. He considered calling Cee Jay back, then decided against it, at least for the time being.

He got out of the car and went around to the rear of the building. As he came toward the porch, a tall string bean of a guy rose from the bench he had been sitting on. "How are you doing, Mr. Callister?" The guy offered Tree his hand. He wore an Armani sports jacket over a crisp white collarless shirt.

It took Tree a moment to realize this was Tommy Dobbs. The last time Tree saw Tommy, he was a reporter for *The Island Reporter* with a pale complexion, pimples, and a lousy wardrobe. This new version of Tommy Dobbs came with a healthy complexion, no pimples, and an impressive wardrobe.

"Tommy," Tree said. "What happened?"

Tommy smiled and showed off a straight line of gleaming white teeth. "Let's just say I learned to separate my whites from my darks—among other things."

One of Tree's complaints about Tommy when he worked for *The Island Reporter* was that, like most young single men, he tended to throw all his laundry into a wash, leaving him with gray, colorless clothes.

"Thought I'd drop around and say hello."

"That's great," Tree said. "It's good to see you. The last time I saw you, you'd just been downsized, and you were on your way to live with your parents."

"Yeah, it wasn't a very good time, that's for sure," Tommy said. "But things have turned around since then."

"So it seems. I hardly recognized you. What are you doing now?"

"Well, sir, as it happens, I'm working for *The Chicago Sun-Times.*"

Tree looked at him in amazement. "You're kidding. That's my old newspaper."

"Yes, I know," Tommy said. "The fact you used to work for the *Sun-Times* inspired me to go to Chicago and try my luck there. It turned out pretty well."

"You got a job at the *Sun-Times?*"

"I've been working for them about a year now."

"That's terrific, Tommy. Working at the *Sun-Times.* Well, what do you know about that? Did you use my name to get an interview?"

"No, as it turned out. They liked some of the stuff I wrote from here."

"So what are you doing back on the island? Are you on vacation?"

"No, I'm not on vacation."

"You're here for a story?"

"That's right," Tommy said.

"Great," Tree said. "A travel piece on Sanibel Island. I've thought about doing that for the *Sun-Times* myself. After all, this is a fascinating place and you certainly know it well, having worked around here."

"I'm not doing a travel piece," Tommy said.

"Oh. Okay." Tree looked confused. "What are you working on?"

"I'm doing a story about you, Mr. C."

———

"Actually, I thought a lot about you," Tommy explained, after he and Tree had settled in his office. "When I was down-sized, I went up to Tampa to stay with my parents. I was sitting around feeling sorry for myself, and I couldn't stop thinking about what you said, you know, about me being a good reporter and everything, and I decided that I'd better help myself because no one else was going to.

"Again, I was thinking of you, remembering that you had worked for *The Chicago Sun-Times*. I got in touch with one of the editors there and started doing some freelance pieces for them. Then the editor told me they were looking for something really unusual."

"What's that, Tommy?" Tree said.

"A good reporter. I told them I was their guy. Then I drove up there overnight and went into the office, not thinking I had any chance at all. Well, it turned out they really liked my freelance stuff." Tommy smiled at Tree. "I owe it all to you, Mr. C."

"If you owe it all to me, don't do this story."

"It's one heck of a story, Mr. Callister."

"No it isn't, Tommy. There is no story."

"The government of Tajikistan believes a private detective on Sanibel Island has nine million it says was stolen from the people of their country. I think that's a story."

"I don't have nine million dollars," Tree said. "There is no nine million dollars."

"The government is lying?"

"Yes."

"The Tajikistan government maintains that a former CIA director concocted a scheme to defraud their president of millions. The former CIA director ended up dead, as did his associates in the conspiracy. But the money never has been recovered."

"The money was recovered."

"Well, yes, they found five hundred thousand dollars. But Tajikistan says there is a lot more that's missing."

"Well, like I say, I don't have it."

"Owen Markfield of the Sanibel-Captiva Police Department thinks you do."

"No matter what he thinks, I don't have it," Tree said. "There's no story."

"I happen to think there is."

"So you think I'm sitting on nine million dollars?"

"There are a lot of unanswered questions around this thing," Tommy said. "If you are innocent, Mr. Callister, you should tell me your side of the story. That would go a long way to reassuring everyone that you don't have the money."

Good grief, Tree thought, how many times during his years as a reporter had he used a similar argument to get people talking? *The story's going to be done, anyway, so it's better if you talk to me, that way you can get your side out.*

Aloud, he said, "All it's going to do is fuel more speculation."

Tommy got to his feet. "It's really good to see you again, Mr. C."

"What does that mean?"

"It means just what I said. It's good to see you. As I explained earlier, I owe you a lot—I owe you everything in fact."

"But you're still going to do this story."

"What would you do if you were in my shoes? That's what I always ask myself when I'm on a story. What would Tree Callister do in a situation like this?"

That left Tree speechless. He knew damned well what he would have done.

"I'm around Sanibel for the next week or so, Mr. C. If you decide you'd like to talk, here's my cellphone number."

He put a card on the desk that said what Tree's card used to say, that here was a reporter from *The Chicago Sun-Times*. Here was a guy who earned a living reporting the news. Here was a young man who had amounted to something.

Tree Callister used to be that same young man. He used to have the power that came from knowing you could decide what was said in print to a large audience about another human being. But not any longer. Now he was one of the powerless, the target of an investigative piece that, depending on how much Tommy was able to uncover, could send him to prison.

There was irony in there somewhere.

"Listen, Tommy—" Tree started to say.

"That's the other thing, Mr. C."

"What's that, Tommy?"

"I'd prefer that you didn't call me Tommy."

"What do you want to be called?"

"I'm Thomas now," he said. "Thomas Dobbs."

Tree bit his tongue.

11

As if he didn't have enough trouble, Tree reflected, swinging the Beetle into the Sanibel School, now he had to deal with his doppelganger, his like self, albeit a sleeker version: Tree wasn't nearly so cleaned up when he was Tommy's age. Or should he now say Thomas?

The circular drive in front of the school was crowded with four buses and the vehicles driven by parents in line to pick up their children—Parent Pickup, as it was called, PPU. Ahead of him a mother loaded two children into the back of her Dodge SUV, and pulled away. Tree moved up just as Marcello came ambling out, accompanied by three boys, trailed by a couple of girls, everyone listening intently as Marcello chattered away. Marcello, *the man*, Tree thought. He couldn't help but smile. The kid knew how to handle himself, that was for sure. A lot better than Tree Callister did when he was that age. Tree was a skinny, unpopular nerd. Girls would not have gone near him, let alone trail him around.

As soon as he saw Tree, Marcello left his friends and came to the Beetle. "I thought we'd get your bike and then I'd give you a ride home," Tree said.

"Sure," Marcello said. "What's up?"

"What do you have to do, tell your bus driver?"

"Yeah, give me a minute." Tree watched Marcello stroll over to the yellow school bus parked at the end of the drive. He returned a moment later, unslinging his backpack before getting into the passenger seat.

"Make sure you do up your seatbelt," Tree said.

Marcello grappled with the seatbelt, cocking his head toward the radio as Elvis sang "Love Me Tender." "They must have given you the radio that only plays that Elvis crap."

"See?" Tree said. "You're getting to know who he is."

"You're corrupting my hearing, man," Marcello said. "What's more, you're not telling me the truth about why you picked me up."

"Give me the directions back to your place," Tree said.

"Man, it's been so long since you had anything to do with me, you can't even remember where I live," Marcello said.

"I just want to make sure we don't get lost," Tree said.

"It's on Sea Oats Drive," Marcello said. "You turn right off San-Cap onto Rabbit Road."

"So we drive past Madison and Joshua's place."

"You got that right," Marcello said.

They drove to Andy Rosse Lane and retrieved Marcello's bike from the garage—Tree having a time jamming it into the back seat.

They started off again, caught in the late afternoon traffic along San-Cap Road. Eventually, Tree was able to turn off onto Rabbit Road and the roadway leading to number five fifty-five. He drove the car up to the house and parked. Marcello looked at him. "What are we doing here?" he demanded.

"I thought we might take a look around."

"Don't know that there's anything to see."

"That's okay," Tree said. "I'm supposed to keep an eye on the place, remember?"

"For a minute there, I forgot they bought you, man."

Outside the car, Tree stretched his sciatic leg. A late afternoon breeze rustled at the nearby palm trees. The house loomed silently above them. Tree stared up at it. Now that he knew it was occupied by an individual who was the *sub-ject* as Cee Jay would say, of a federal investigation, it was perhaps time to look at the house from a different perspective.

"So what are you looking for?" Marcello, impatient with the dog work of private detection.

Tree took his eyes off the house and focused on Marcello. "You never told me how you met Madison and Joshua."

Marcello shrugged and said, "The ad."

"What ad?"

"The ad I put up on Facebook saying that the Sanibel Sunset Detective Agency was looking for clients. Reasonable rates, I said."

"You advertised on Facebook?"

"What? You don't have a Facebook page?"

Tree rolled his eyes. "And that's when Joshua and Madison got in touch with you?"

"Among the others, yeah," Marcello said.

Tree looked at him in surprise. "There were others?"

"All sorts of kids are after my services."

"You're kidding. Why would kids your age need a private detective?"

"Same kind of stuff adults need detectives for. A lot of parents, they're watching their kids, right? You know, video surveillance, Internet monitoring, parental controls on TV and computers. It's endless. But what do kids know about their parents? They don't know jack when it comes down to it. So a lot of kids want to know more."

"But how are you planning to get around town so you can investigate parents?" Tree said.

"That's where you come in," Marcello said.

"Marcello, I don't come into this at all."

"The partnership I've been telling you about."

"How many times do I have to tell you? There is no partnership," Tree said.

"Then how come you picked me up at school? What are we doing here?"

"Just because I picked you up at school, doesn't mean we're partners."

"It means you need me, man. Means you *need* a partner."

"So here's what we're going to do," Tree said. "We're going to look through their garbage."

"What?" Marcello sounded appalled.

"Their garbage—*partner.*"

"Why we doing that?"

"That's what detectives are supposed to do," Tree said.

"Detectives don't do that," Marcello said disdainfully.

"They do if they're looking for clues."

Marcello groaned loudly but then dutifully trailed Tree behind the house where they found a garbage bin. No one had bothered to lock down the plastic lids. Tree lifted one of the lids to reveal two garbage cans stuffed with green plastic trash bags. Tree yanked one of the bags out and placed it on the ground beside the bin. A twist tie held the top of the bag closed. Tree undid it and opened the bag. From the look of the potpourri of waste inside, Ryde Bodie didn't believe in recycling. Marcello peered in the bag and made a face, "What a mess," he said.

"Welcome to the exciting world of private investigation," Tree said.

"I'm not going through that," Marcello said, backing away.

"You're the one who wanted to be a detective, remember? Open one of the other bags, and poke through it, see what you can find."

Marcello seemed to steel himself before lifting out another garbage bag. Tree turned his attention to the bag before him, gingerly moving aside a filter soaked with coffee grinds. Aha! He thought. Ryde Bodie drinks coffee. Probably in the morning. He also blows his nose with good quality tissues—or his kids do. What else? Old newspapers and copies of *Time* magazine. A Target bag full of shredded paper. Ryde took the time to destroy documents he did not want people poking through his garbage to see. Three other Target bags were full of similarly shredded paper.

Tree looked over at Marcello. He stood poised over his open garbage bag, peering down into it, unmoving.

"How are you doing?" Tree called.

"I don't like this," Marcello said.

Tree went back to his bag, clawing through old newspapers—the *Island Sun, The New York Times, The Fort Myers News Press,* and, this was interesting, a Spanish language newspaper, *El Universal.* What was Ryde Bodie doing reading Mexican newspapers? From the sticker attached to the paper's front page, Ryde had the paper sent to him. Not to the Rabbit Road address, however. The paper was addressed to him at WGE International LLC, care of the Santini Marina Plaza, Unit #5, Fort Myers Beach, Fl.

WGE—could that stand for Wayne Granger Enterprises?

Tree tore off the corner of the newspaper containing the address just as a car wheeled into view. Marcello's head jerked up from the garbage bag he had been staring at. The car came to a stop and a heavyset man struggled out from behind the wheel. He saw Tree and his face twisted into anger.

"Son of a bitch!" he yelled, starting toward Tree.

The man waved the single black flower he was holding as he came to a halt inches from where Tree more or less stood his ground. He thrust his flat Midwestern face at Tree demanding, "Where's Granger?"

Tree said, "I have no idea."

The man held up the flower. "I got this delivered this morning. What the hell is that supposed to mean?"

"I have no idea," Tree said.

The heavyset man looked exasperated. "It's an iris," the man said. "I had to look it up. A *black* iris. Who sends me a black iris? No note, no nothing. Is this Granger's doing?"

Tree said, "I'm afraid you've got the wrong guy. I'm not associated with Granger."

The angry man was not deterred. "You're standing in his yard, you're putting out his garbage, and you claim you don't know him? Don't give me that crap!"

"I'm a private detective," Tree said. "I'm looking into the man you call Granger."

The man squinted at him. "You're a private dick?"

"Here, I can show you," Tree said, pulling out his wallet. He opened it and withdrew the license issued to him by the State of Florida. Tree noticed Marcello staring up at him, eyes wide and unblinking. The heavyset man took the license from Tree and peered at it. He looked at Marcello. "You take a kid along with you when you're working?"

"I'm his partner," Marcello announced.

"What the hell's going on?" the man said. The blustery air appeared to seep out of him. "I need my money. My wife's very sick. Very, very sick. We're in a tough spot, I can tell you."

"I'm sorry," Tree said. "What did you say your name was?"

"I didn't say, but it's Waterhouse. Jim Waterhouse. I tell you, I don't like this black iris crap. It's creepy. The bastard promised me twenty per cent return on my investment, and instead I get a flower? Something is wrong that's for sure."

"What investment? What are you talking about?"

"Come on, if you're a detective investigating him, you must know what I'm talking about."

"Remind me."

"These high-interest motor vehicle retail installment contracts," Waterhouse said. "Twenty per cent return, Granger promised. Guaranteed, he said. Only I haven't seen a cent, and now I can't get hold of Granger. You say you're a private dick? You got any idea where he is?"

Tree shook his head, "Sorry. As I explained to you, I'm trying to find out more about him myself. How did you know Granger lived here?"

Waterhouse's face darkened again. "To hell with this," he announced. "To hell with it all. I'll take care of this my own way."

"I'm not sure what you're getting at," Tree said.

"The rain's gonna come down on Granger if he doesn't handle this and handle it soon. You tell him that, understand what I'm saying?"

"No, Jim, I don't understand what you're saying."

"The rain's coming down, you tell him that. You make sure he knows."

Jim Waterhouse stomped away to his car, got in, and sped off.

12

I don't understand what's going on," Marcello said as Tree drove him home.

"I'm not sure I understand, either," Tree said.

"Like this dude's been ripped off, is that it?"

"He thinks he's been ripped off, that's for certain," Tree said.

"Told you this guy Granger was up to no good."

"Yeah, but Marcello, there's a big difference between someone who's unhappy with a business deal and a father who is placing his children in jeopardy."

"What's the difference?" Marcello demanded. "You tell me that. Dude's bad with business, he's bad with his kids."

The unassailable logic of thirteen-year-old detectives, Tree thought.

"You gotta do something," Marcello said. "They're in trouble, like I've been telling you all along."

Yes, do something, Tree thought. But do what, exactly?

Marcello lived in a frame bungalow on Sea Oats Drive. Jennifer Lake, an attractive African American woman in her late forties, stood on the front lawn wearing a worried expression as they drove up. Tree waved to her as he brought the car to a stop. She did not wave back.

"How are you doing, Jennifer?"

"Well, I'll tell you, I don't like it much when you pick up Marcello from school and don't tell me in advance."

"I'm sorry about that," Tree said. "I should have called."

"It's all right," Marcello said. "Tree and I are partners."

Jennifer Lake didn't look as if that was all right at all.

———————

To Tree's surprise, Freddie's Mercedes was in the drive when he arrived home. He couldn't believe it. She wasn't supposed to be back for another two days. He hurried inside and found her, still business casual from the Chicago trip, blond elegance unruffled, forever his green-eyed beauty, in the midst of pouring a glass of chardonnay.

"I just got in," she said a moment before she put the wine bottle down and flung herself into his arms and kissed him so hard it left him breathless. "I missed you," she said between kisses.

Tree said, "Can't tell you how much I missed you."

"Show don't tell," she admonished, taking him by the hand and leading him into the bedroom, shedding business casual. For the next forty minutes or so they eagerly demonstrated to each other how young and energetic they remained.

Afterward, they snuggled together, luxuriating in each other's warmth, delighted to be reunited.

The meetings in Chicago had gone well, she said. The investors involved in the syndicate that had purchased the five Dayton supermarkets in the South Florida area were happy enough, and the stores were holding their own despite the difficult economic climate and the continuing pressures from the big box competition provided by the Targets and the Wal-Marts.

As for what Tree had been up to, well, that was a little more problematic, wasn't it? But then what Tree was doing with his life since they had moved to Captiva defied rational description. How to explain, for example, a sixtyish former newspaper reporter who takes on two children as clients and then gets caught red-handed watching their father's house, only to be hired by the father to—well, watch the house? Watching for what? Federal agents who might come calling because the father, a smiling charmer if there ever was one, has two names, is rather sketchy about what he does for a living, and is the subject of an investigation?

Freddie took all this in lying next to her husband. When he finished outlining recent events, she said, "Let me get this straight. His kids say their father has one name, Wayne Granger, while he introduces himself as someone else entirely."

"Ryde Bodie."

"Wayne Granger is also the name of this fellow who confronted you on Rabbit Road—"

"Jim Waterhouse."

"Jim Waterhouse was looking for Wayne Granger?"

"That's right."

"Because he believes Granger has defrauded him."

"Selling him something called high-interest motor vehicle retail installment contracts. Have you ever heard of those?"

"No," Freddie said. "But that doesn't mean anything."

"Waterhouse said he was supposed to be getting a twenty per cent return on his investment, and hadn't got it."

"Maybe that's why the feds are investigating Wayne Granger who is also Ryde Bodie."

"That's what I'm thinking," Tree agreed.

"His children may be onto something," Freddie said. "None of this sounds right."

Tree had to concede it didn't.

By now it was dark, and Tree must have dozed off because the next thing he knew Freddie was prodding him and calling, "Tree. Tree, wake up."

He sat up and immediately saw what Freddie saw, light flickering eerily against the bedroom wall. "What do you suppose that is?" Freddie said.

Tree got out of bed and went over to the sliding glass doors that led onto the terrace. He stepped outside and saw that the night sky was lit in a fiery glow. Freddie was behind him, putting her hand on his shoulder. "A fire," she said.

"Yeah, but where's it coming from?"

They went inside, got dressed to the distant sound of fire engine sirens, and then hurried over to Captiva Drive. The fire glow was coming from further down. It lit the night sky, intersected by plumes of rising black smoke. Other onlookers gathered at the intersection of Andy Rosse and Captiva, peering down the road, speculating as to what might have caught fire.

"It's got to be one of the houses on Captiva," someone said, and everyone murmured agreement—and suddenly Tree had an inkling of what was burning. He turned and ran back to the house. He got behind the wheel of the Beetle, started up the engine and backed out onto Andy Rosse Lane.

He caught a glimpse of an astonished-looking Freddie as he whipped past. The roadway soon became choked with fire trucks and police and emergency vehicles, lights flashing in the night.

A sheriff's deputy waved him over to the beach side of the road. Tree parked on the shoulder and got out. Flames leapt above the wall surrounding the Traven house. The fire burned furiously, fed by a strong ocean breeze, flames licking at the windows and breaking through the roof.

"Hey, Mr. Callister."

Tree turned to find Tommy Dobbs standing behind him, the fire lighting his pale face.

"Tommy," Tree said. "What brings you out here?"

"Thomas, Mr. Callister."

"Right. Thomas."

"I'm a reporter. Reporters cover fires, don't they?"

"Yes, I suppose they do," Tree said.

"Must be something to see this place burning," Thomas said.

"Why do you say that?"

"You know, from when the Travens lived here. Doesn't it bring back memories?"

"In your role as reporter covering the fire, have you spoken to the police or fire fighters?"

"Of course," Tommy said with a smile. "They were very impressed that a reporter from Chicago would be here. A couple of these guys, particularly the cops, remember me from when I worked for *The Islander.*"

"Do they know what caused the fire?"

"No idea as yet, but they've found something."

"What's that?"

"A body, Mr. C."

Tree's heart jumped. "Did they say who it was?"

Tommy shook his head. "A charred corpse was all they said."

Ryder Bodie who was also known as Wayne Granger? Tree wondered.

13

At six the next morning, Tree prepared Freddie's coffee and turned on WGCU. The station didn't have much new about the fire other than to report that the mansion once owned by the disgraced media mogul Brand Traven had been destroyed the night before, and that a body had been found in the remains. Police and fire officials had not yet released the victim's identity. They were not saying anything about the cause of the fire, either.

"But it could be this Ryde Bodie," Freddie said, appearing in the kitchen simply chic by Eileen Fisher.

"He said he was leaving town with his kids."

"Did he say where—or leave you a cellphone number?"

Tree shook his head, silently kicking himself for not getting more information from Ryde.

"You drove off like a crazy fool last night."

"I'm sorry about that," Tree said.

"All your dreams gone up in smoke," Freddie said, pouring herself coffee.

"No, just a client's house—after the client hired me to keep an eye on it—the client whose burnt corpse they may have found in the remains."

Freddie, coffee in hand, turned to face Tree. "You're not blaming yourself for what happened, are you?"

Tree shook his head. "I guess not, no."

"Tree there's nothing you could have done."

Tree said, "Do you remember Tommy Dobbs, the reporter for *The Islander*?"

"Is he back on Sanibel working for *The Islander*?"

"Well, he's back but he's not working for *The Islander.*"

"Who is he working for?" Freddie sipped at her coffee.

"The *Sun-Times* in Chicago, if you can believe it."

"Good for him," Freddie said. "Was he covering the fire?"

"He was there, but that's not what he's writing about," Tree said.

"What's he writing about?"

Tree took a deep breath before he said, "Me."

Freddie stared at him. "Why would he be doing a story about you?"

"It's that nine million dollars."

Freddie closed her eyes momentarily, opened them, and then carefully put her coffee cup on the counter. "I'd better get to work," she said.

"Freddie, I don't have nine million dollars. There was no nine million."

"You know what, Tree?" Freddie said. "I believe you. The trouble is no one else does."

"There are those who remain unconvinced, no question," Tree admitted.

"Do you want to know why?"

He looked at her.

"No one believes you're telling the whole truth about your involvement with the late Elizabeth Traven, that's why."

"What about you, Freddie? Do you think I'm telling the truth?"

"You shouldn't ask me that, Tree," she said. "You might get an answer you don't like."

Well, he thought, she's right about that.

———————

"I know a couple of guys over at the fire department," Todd Jackson said. "They talk about the fire triangle—three factors that are necessary to create fire."

"And I'm going to bet you can tell us what those three factors are," Rex Baxter said.

"Oxygen, a fuel source, and heat," Todd explained in his best teacher-student voice. "For the fire to sustain itself, the oxygen level must be above sixteen per cent. The fuel can be any flammable substance, and the heat can come from something as simple as a match. For arson to be present one or more parts of the fire triangle must have been tampered with."

"And is that what they are saying happened in this case?" Tree asked.

"The guys at the department tell me a couple of things—indications there were a number of points of origin and also the presence of an accelerant, in this case, gasoline cans found near the dead guy's body."

Tree finished his coffee. "Do they have any idea who the man is?"

"The body was pretty badly burned—charred is the word my guys are using. But they think it might have been the owner, trying to burn down his new house for the insurance—but then he got caught in his own fire and died."

Tree looked at Rex. "You know Ryder Bodie owns the place."

"That would mean we're going to have to start looking for a replacement for the Oscar show," Rex said.

"Boy, Rex," Todd said, "you really are a heartless character. The guy may be dead and you're worried about your Oscar show."

"I am a show business professional," Rex said archly. "No matter what happens, the show must go on." He shrugged. "Besides, I have sources, too, and they tell me not to jump to conclusions before we have all the facts. That way we won't unnecessarily kill off any island residents or hurt tourism. Usually, we have Tree here to screw up business but so far this year he's been unusually quiet."

"So far," Todd said. "Let's not underestimate Tree. The season is far from over."

"I'm trying to convince him to move down to Naples," Rex said. "Destroy tourism there for a while."

Tree said, "Ryde has two children."

"How do you know that?" said Rex.

"I've met them. Madison and Joshua. If it was Ryde who died in the fire last night, the kids are orphans."

"That place is cursed if you ask me," Rex said. "If there is such a thing as a haunted house on Sanibel Island, that's it."

A tired-looking Detective Owen Markfield appeared in the doorway. Tree could see Cee Jay Boone behind him. "Good morning," Markfield said. Everyone stared at him. The detective trained his gaze on Tree. "Callister, I wonder if we might have a word with you."

"What's this about?" Tree said.

Markfield stepped further into the office and said to Rex and Todd, "Gentlemen, would you excuse us?"

Rex said to Tree, "Maybe you should have someone present when you talk to this guy."

"Maybe like a lawyer," Todd Jackson added, glancing at Cee Jay who remained parked in the doorway.

"It's all right," Tree said. "Detectives Markfield and Boone are old friends."

Neither police officer said anything.

"They don't look like old friends to me," Rex said.

"We just have a few questions," Cee Jay said.

Rex got to his feet and Todd followed. "If you need me, Tree, I'm downstairs," Rex said. He gave Cee Jay and

Markfield a dark look. "Just remember, Tree here is a proud member of the chamber," as though that was all the protection anyone on Sanibel would ever need.

"Yeah, I'll keep that in mind," Markfield said dryly.

"I'll see you later, Tree," Todd said.

Once Rex and Todd left, Tree invited the detectives to sit down. Markfield made himself comfortable in the chair recently vacated by Rex. Cee Jay, however, did not move from the doorway.

"We wanted to ask you about the fire at the Traven house last night," Cee Jay said.

"I didn't set it, if that's what you mean," Tree said.

Neither detective smiled.

Markfield said, "But you were present."

"Me and the dozens of others in the neighborhood who came to see what the commotion was about."

Markfield said, "Before that, Callister, do you mind telling us where you were?"

"I was at home in bed with my wife," Tree said.

"Can anyone other than your wife verify that?" Markfield said.

"Wouldn't you know it? The only other person in bed with me last night was my wife."

By now, Markfield had out the notebook he always seemed to bring along for Tree Callister interrogations. Those notebooks filled up fast. Markfield scribbled a notation with his pen.

"You're kidding," Tree said looking at the detectives. "You don't seriously think I'm a suspect in this, do you?"

"Suspect in what?" Markfield demanded.

"I understand the fire might have been set intentionally," Tree said.

"What would make you think that?"

"Why else would you be here?" Tree said.

"Are you familiar with the person who now owns the Traven place?" This from Cee Jay.

"I've met the guy," Tree said.

"This would be Ryder Bodie."

Tree hesitated before he said, "That's correct." He wondered if Cee Jay knew that Ryde Bodie was also Wayne Granger—the subject of that federal investigation she had mentioned. He decided not to say anything.

"Is that who you found in the house?"

Markfield and Cee Jay traded quick glances. "We have yet to make a positive identification of the body," Cee Jay said.

Markfield said, "Where did you meet Bodie?"

"At the Big Arts Center."

Markfield jotted something into his notebook and then looked up at Tree. "Did he ask you to do anything for him?"

"He hired me to keep an eye on the place," Tree said.

"He didn't hire you to help him set the fire?"

Tree looked at Markfield. "You've got to be kidding."

Cee Jay said, "Just answer the question, Tree."

"No, he didn't," Tree said.

"Suppose I was to tell you we think he did," Markfield said.

"Let me see. First of all I'm stealing nine million dollars from foreign governments. Now I'm setting fire to mansions on Captiva Drive. I'm a real master crook, aren't I?"

"You're forgetting the part where you kill people," Markfield said.

"Only because I know you'll always remind me," Tree said.

That reduced the room to silence. Finally, Cee Jay straightened up from the door and said, "You are aware that Ryde Bodie is also known as Wayne Granger?"

Tree looked at her. "Yes, I'm aware of that."

Cee Jay didn't meet Tree's gaze. Instead she looked over at Markfield, who shrugged before rising to his feet.

"You're not thinking of leaving the area, are you Tree?" Markfield said.

"Should I be thinking about that?"

"That's the point," Markfield said. "You shouldn't be thinking about it. You should be staying right where you are."

"I'll give it some thought," Tree said.

14

When you think you can go further along Estero Boulevard without driving right off Fort Myers Beach, that's when the Santini Marina Plaza pops up. It is a low-slung salmon-colored mall fronting a marina and a boat storage facility.

Tree turned into the parking lot and nudged the Beetle into a space adjacent to a Bank of America cash machine where at mid-day the real-money diehards lined up. He got out and went along a walkway packed with residents of a certain age arriving for lunch from the surrounding condo towers. He passed Annette's Book Nook, and a real estate office where a knot of tourists studied the condo listings mounted behind glass on the wall.

Unit five was located a couple of doors beyond the real estate office. There was nothing to indicate this was the office of WGE International. Instead, curtains were drawn across the plate glass windows on either side of the locked glass entrance door. He peered through the door, but could see no more than the outlines of a shadowy interior.

He went back to the Book Nook and poked his head in the door. A willowy woman seated behind a desk, surrounded by shelves choked with books, examined him from behind rimless glasses. "I was supposed to meet someone at number five. But there doesn't seem to be anyone there."

"I never see anyone in there," the woman said. "I don't think the place is occupied. You sure it's number five?"

"I'd better phone and check," Tree said. "Thanks."

Tree walked around to where the iron girders of the boat storage units formed an ugly barrier between the plaza and the marina. He ducked through the ironwork of the storage facility and came out onto a paved roadway. Beyond the roadway, a series of T-shaped docks jutted into the bay. At the top of one of the Ts, a long, sleek yacht glinted in the morning sun—*el Trueno*, according to the lettering stenciled in black vinyl across the stern

On the dock, a man, stripped to the waist, his gut bulging over his shorts, aimed a hose at the yacht's hull. Water from the hose splashed against the hull's ivory surface sending a hazy rainbow into the air. The man turned and saw Tree standing there. He had black hair and a matching mustache. It was, Tree realized, Diego, the guy who had accosted Ryde Bodie at the Traven mansion. He did not smile when he saw Tree—or appear to recognize him.

"Beautiful afternoon," Tree said.

The black-haired man named Diego just stared and didn't say anything. After a moment, he turned back to the much more important business of spraying the hull with water.

Tree debated whether to say something about having met him before, but decided that was not a good idea. Instead, he walked back to the plaza and made his way along to the Sandbar and Grille. A half dozen weathered old salts sat on wrought iron chairs finishing lunch. Tree said good afternoon, and everyone responded enthusiastically. A stranger had arrived to hopefully add a little spice to the normal unfolding of another routine day in paradise.

Tree said, "Anybody here own a boat at the marina?"

Three of the men nodded. One of the men who didn't nod grinned and said, "That's why we make nice to these characters, so they'll take us out fishing every once in a while."

"The best way to enjoy a boat," a fellow with a lot of front teeth missing, said. "Make sure the *other* guy owns the boat."

"Looking for a place to keep a boat?" The question came from an elderly man with a full head of russet-colored hair.

"Not me, but a friend of mine is looking around," Tree said. "He's at a place just off Sanibel, but he's not very happy there."

"Fine spot here," the russet-haired man said. "Rates are good, and I think spaces are available. Pretty good draft, too, depending on the size of your boat."

"My friend's boat is a good size. Not as big as that yacht parked down there."

"You mean *el Trueno*?" said the russet-haired man.

"That's the one," Tree said.

"Means thunder in Spanish. Out of Miami."

"I guess if the marina can take a boat like that, it could handle my friend's boat okay."

The russet-haired guy lifted his beer bottle. "That's what you're after," he said. "You think one of us owns that gorgeous boat. You're hoping to make friends with us so you get invited out for a ride and maybe a glass or two of champagne thrown in, poured by a lovely in one of those string bikinis. I get it."

The group laughed, including Tree. "Red," the guy with the missing teeth said to the russet-haired guy, "you wouldn't even know how to get that baby out of the bay."

"Couple of more beers, no problem," Red said, inducing more easy laughter.

"Do you know who owns it?" Tree asked.

Everyone shook their heads. "Whoever it is, isn't very friendly," Red said. "Just goes to show you, the bigger the boat, the more miserable it makes you."

"Mexican, three or four of them, including this tiny, ugly woman," the guy with the missing teeth said.

"Ugly isn't the word for it," Red said,

"I thought they didn't speak English, and that's why they were so withdrawn," the no-teeth guy said. "But I think they speak the lingo all right."

"There's a fellow with black hair and a mustache down there now," Tree said.

"Yeah, I saw him this morning," said Red. "He's one of 'em all right. Miserable cuss. But I don't think he's the owner."

An elegant man with a shock of fine white hair pushed the remnants of his burger to one side and said, "The kids are kind of sweet, though."

"There are kids on the yacht?"

"A boy and a girl," Red said. "Bored, hanging around, no one to play with."

"Is the yacht here all the time?" Tree asked.

Red shrugged. "Just for the past two weeks. It comes and goes. A day, couple of days, and then it's gone again."

"What about the kids?" Tree said. "Are they always on-board?"

"I've only seen them a couple of times," Red said. He looked around at the others, and the group nodded agreement.

"Mostly, it's been these thug-like characters," said the elegant man. "Interesting types, but they do make you wonder."

"Wonder about what?" Red said.

"Maybe along the lines of what's happening to the world."

"Well, we know what's happening," Red said. "It's going to hell."

Everyone laughed.

That's when Tree spotted Tommy—Thomas—Dobbs coming toward him. He couldn't believe it. What was he doing out here?

Tommy wore a white shirt and a tie, the tie askew as befitted a proper Chicago newsman—the way Tree used to wear it back in the days when a tie was part of a reporter's uniform.

Tree felt his irritation level rise, but he forced himself to remain calm. He thanked the men around the table and walked to meet Tommy.

"If I didn't know better, I would say you are following me."

"I am following you, Mr. C."

"So quit following me."

"Then help me get my story," Tommy said.

"There is no story, and if there was, this certainly isn't the way to get me to tell it."

"Please explain to me what you're doing here, Mr. Callister."

"No."

"Are you on a case?"

Tree went past Tommy and proceeded to his car. Tommy followed him saying, "You know the police suspect you may have set that fire last night."

"I wonder who put that notion into their heads." Tree reached the Beetle and unlocked the door.

Tommy arranged to look shocked. "You don't think I had anything to do with that, do you?"

"How else would they have known I was at the fire?"

"How come you lock your door?" Tommy said.

Tree looked at him blankly.

"You're driving a convertible, Mr. C. The top's down. Why lock your door?"

"I'm from Chicago," Tree said. "Everyone locks everything. It's the Chicago way."

Tree opened the door and started into the car.

Tommy said, "At least let me buy you a cup of coffee, Mr. C. Make amends."

"Make amends? You're going to buy me a coffee to make amends?"

Tommy produced an embarrassed grin. "I'm on sort of a restricted budget."

That stopped Tree. The light went abruptly on. "You're not working for the *Sun-Times*, are you Tommy?"

"For Pete's sake, Mr. Callister, it's *Thomas*." His anger was edged with desperation. "How many times do I have to tell you that?"

"You haven't been telling me the truth." Tree, pressing.

"I *am* working for them." His vehemence seemed to knock the air out of him. "It's just that I'm not really, truly on staff. At least not yet."

"Not yet? What's that mean?"

"It means I really need this story, Mr. Callister. If they like it, they'll use it, and that's the foot in the door I need. You know how it is. You need that one break—and you could help me get it."

Tree closed the car door and leaned against the Beetle. "You know, Tommy—Thomas—it would help if you would start out telling me the truth. That way I wouldn't have to waste all this time with you lying and me having to stop to figure out that you are lying."

"I was telling you the truth—sort of."

"It's the 'sort of' part that you have trouble with," Tree said.

"You gotta help me, Mr. Callister."

"I keep telling you, there's no story."

"You got nine million bucks for God's sake!" Tommy shouted. "There's a story!"

A couple on their way into the Book Nook stopped to look at them. Tree said, "Calm down will you?"

Tommy lowered his head. "Sorry, Mr. Callister. I'm kind of at the end of my rope here."

That had the effect of making Tree feel remorseful about the manner in which he was treating Tommy.

"You're putting me in a terrible position," he said.

"I understand that."

"You may get a job, but I could potentially get myself into a lot of trouble I don't need right now."

"So there *is* a story." Tommy sounded triumphant, as if clever questioning had finally elicited the information he was looking for.

Tree said, "Tell me this: are you a good enough reporter that you can get me the name of the corpse they found at the Traven house last night?"

"Sure, I could do that."

"Then do it. After that, we can talk."

"So you'll help me, is that what you're saying?"

"Get me that name, and I'll do the best I can," Tree said.

"I don't know," Tommy said. "That doesn't sound like much of a deal to me."

Tree looked at his watch. "I'm late for rehearsal."

"Rehearsal?" Thomas looked mystified.

"I'm in a show at Big Arts, and I've got to get over there."

"So we've got a deal?"

"Get me a name," Tree said, getting behind the wheel. The last thing he saw as he backed out, was Tommy, shoulders slumped dejectedly, looking lost and alone. Tree swore he was not going to feel sorry for him.

15

On his way back to Sanibel, Tree phoned Freddie. "What's up?" she said, her tone business professional at this time of the day.

"Have you got a moment?"

"I'm going into as meeting in about ten minutes, my love," Freddie said, momentarily more the loving partner than the business professional.

"Are you near a computer?"

"I'm going to get you an iPad so you can do this yourself," Freddie said.

"This way we get to interact more often," Tree said.

"Is that what we get to do?" Freddie said. "Okay. I'm at the computer."

"See what happens when you Google Wayne Granger Enterprises International," Tree said.

There was a moment of silence. Tree could hear Freddie's fingers striking a keyboard. Then: "I get nothing."

"Try high-interest motor vehicle retail installment contracts."

"Just a moment," she said. He could hear her fingers working the keyboard. She came back on the line. "Here's something. There's a *Wally Garrison* who ran a company called Wally Garrison Enterprises International. Apparently Wally became rich flogging motor vehicle contracts to his clients."

"That has to be the WGE I'm looking for," Tree said.

"Hold on," Freddie said. "There's a story in Forbes magazine. Here's what it says: 'As the president and sole shareholder of WGE International, an investment company, Wally could make you rich, provided you were Wally's friend. Therefore, a lot of people became friends with Wally—not to mention enthusiastic investors.

"'Wonderful Wally, as he came to be known, involved his friends in something a little different—motor vehicle retail installment contracts. Not very sexy, you think? Well, think again. You see, most car loans at new car dealers are done via a motor vehicle retail installment contract. These contracts, or notes, can be bundled and purchased using investors' money. In turn, the investors are guaranteed a hefty twenty per cent return. Wonderful Wally's pals couldn't lose.

"'Except they could. Wonderful Wally kept all the plates spinning at WGE via an age-old ploy used by fraudsters like him—older investors got that twenty per cent return, using the investment money he had taken from newcomers.'"

"In other words, a Ponzi scheme," Tree said.

"You took the words right out of my mouth," Freddie said.

"Keep going."

"Okay, apparently Wally had had to learn what all spinners of plates and Ponzi schemers learn, that the plates can't keep spinning forever. In Wally's case according to this story, they came crashing down in the wake of the economic meltdown of 2008. Suddenly, Wally's friends wanted their money out from WGE and those high-interest auto contracts. Except, of course, there was no money. Most of it had gone to fuel the lavish lifestyle of Wonderful Wally.

"The article goes on to say that as a result of the meltdown, Wonderful Wally was no longer so wonderful. He suddenly didn't have so many friends. In fact, he didn't have any friends."

"That's when the feds entered the picture," Tree said.

"Exactly. The U.S. Attorney's Office charged him with conspiracy to commit mail and wire fraud. Basically, the auto contracts were either worthless—multiple investors had purchased the same contracts sometimes as many as four times—or they were non-existent: the investor was paying money for contracts Wally never bought.

"The story says that if Wally had been convicted on the fraud charges, he would have gone to jail for thirty years. But Wally never got to trial."

"What happened to him?"

"Soon after being indicted, he was found dead in his ten million dollar home in suburban Charlotte. At the time the story was printed, police had not released a cause of death, but they weren't suspecting foul play. Does that help you?"

"No mention of Wayne Granger or Ryde Bodie?"

"Nothing comes up in connection with Wonderful Wally," Freddie said.

———————

By the time Tree reached the Big Arts Center, he was running fifteen minutes late, thanks to the traffic coming off Fort Myers Beach and then more congestion getting onto Sanibel Island. The rest of the cast were already present, chatting in huddles or occupying seats in the theater studying their lines. Rex stood near the front, frowning. "All right everyone," he said as Tree entered the theater, "Tree is finally here. Let's get started."

When Tree approached Rex, he saw a familiar figure coming toward him. Ryder Bodie plastered one of his blast furnace grins on his handsome face and had a handshake ready. "Tree, good to see you again." He pumped Tree's hand.

All Tree could say was, "You're alive."

"Alive? Of course I'm alive. What else would I be?"

"Dead. In last night's fire."

Ryde shook his head. "I told you I had business off Sanibel. Got in first thing this morning."

"I thought you were gone for two weeks."

"That was the plan," Ryde said. "But something came up."

"Like your house burning down?" Tree said.

"Besides, I couldn't miss the show, could I?"

"What about the kids? Are they with you?"

"Of course. Where else would they be?"

"And they're okay?"

Ryde gave him a quizzical look. "Never been better."

"All right, everyone," Rex announced. "Let's begin our run-through, see what we've got."

Ryde slapped Tree's arm with the script he was holding. "This is gonna be fun. No business like show business, right Tree?"

Tree said, "You're sure you're okay?"

"Sure. Why wouldn't I be?"

"Ryde, your house burned to the ground last night. A lot of people think you're dead,"

"Well, I'm not dead yet, old buddy," Ryde said. "As for the house, it's being taken care of. Not to worry." As if houses burning to the ground were a regular occurrence in his life.

"Not to worry? Listen, the police have been around questioning me."

"Questioning you about what?"

"About the fire."

"Why would the police question you?"

"Among other reasons, because I was there—and they think I helped you start it."

Ryde looked mystified. "What were you doing there?"

"The house was on fire. I was supposed to be looking after the place. Isn't that what you hired me for?"

Ryde said, "Well, I didn't hire you to burn it down."

"I didn't burn it down."

"Good. I hope you told the police that."

"Nonetheless, they seem to think I'm a suspect, along with you."

"But you're not, right?"

"Of course not. Are you?"

"Why would I burn down my own house after all the work I've put into it?"

"Someone died in that fire."

"Probably the jerk who set it." Ryde smiled and patted Tree's arm. "The police will get to the bottom of it, don't worry. Come on, let's rehearse. We've got a show to do."

Rex called out, "Can we please have Bonnie and Ryde, our Fred and Ginger, onstage, so we can run through what they're doing."

Ryde followed Bonnie, a statuesque woman with soft blond hair, onto the stage. The music started up, "The Way You Look Tonight." Ryde twirled Bonnie, not Astaire and Rogers, but graceful enough to impress the Big Arts crowd—and Tree. There was applause from the other cast members as the couple approached the podium and announced the winner of the Best Actor Oscar.

That was Tree's cue to mount the stage. By the time he reached Bonnie and Ryde, he had his speech out and ready.

He read:

"Good grief, they told me to be brief.
But there are so many people who deserve my thanks,
From Steven Spielberg to Tom Hanks.

And I wouldn't be here without my Mom and Dad.
Except they think I'm gay and it makes them sad..."

When he finished, everyone laughed and applauded a beaming Tree. Ryde's eyes twinkled with delight. For some reason that made Tree feel closer to him. Ryde was a kindred spirit up here on stage, encouraging Tree to new performance heights. They would work together with Bonnie, too, of course, and Tree would steal the show on Oscar night. Even Rex seemed pleased. "I wasn't expecting that," he called to Tree from his seat in the theater. "Nicely done. Maybe you won't screw this up, after all."

Tree floated off the stage, wondering again if he should have become an actor instead of wasting all those years in the newspaper business. Ah, well, he thought, wistfully, too late now.

Or maybe not.

There was Ryde Bodie, grinning, squeezing his arm affectionately and saying into his ear: "Well done, Tree. You're a star!"

————

"Did I ever tell you I thought of becoming an actor as a young man?" Tree said later that evening as he and Freddie sat on the terrace by the pool, Freddie sipping the single glass of chardonnay she allowed herself before dinner.

"Let's say you've mentioned it a couple of times lately," Freddie said. She had changed from Eileen Fisher into shorts and T-shirt by Target. "I thought you always wanted to be a newspaperman. I thought when you were a kid, while everyone else around you was floundering, wondering what they were going to do with their lives, you knew exactly what you wanted."

"I actually dreamt of playing rhythm guitar in Elvis's band," Tree said. "For years as a teenager, I fantasized about that."

"Except your fantasy failed to extend to actually learning to play the guitar," Freddie said.

"That's why fantasies are so great. You can imagine without going through the pain of actually having to do anything. But I did think seriously about acting."

"So why didn't you pursue it?"

Tree shrugged. "I guess I took the path of least resistance. People liked what I wrote, and they encouraged me to write more, and before I knew it I had a newspaper job. Nobody ever encouraged me to become an actor."

"You should have said something," Freddie said.

"I suppose it worked out, okay." He smiled at her. "Besides, if I had become an actor that would have changed the trajectory of my life, and I might not have met you."

"Perish the thought," Freddie said.

"I'm serious," Tree said.

She got up and leaned over him and kissed him with wine-scented lips. "You're such a charmer," she murmured. And kissed him again. "I'm going inside to make dinner."

"Do you need any help?"

She shook her head. "You're going to have to suffer through turkey burgers again tonight."

"Fine with me," he said.

They ate on the terrace, the night cooling around them, and they got down to the business of his business, the subject du jour these days, even when they didn't intend it to be. Tree told Freddie about his latest encounter with Ryde Bodie, how he didn't seem at all worried about the fire destroying his house or about the fact that someone had died in the blaze.

"So if Ryde wasn't killed, who was?"

"The police say they have yet to identify the body."

"What about the kids?" Freddie said. "Did he talk about them?"

"He says they're with him, and they're okay."

"But are they? I mean isn't that what this is all about? A boy and a girl scared of their father?"

"Ryde said his wife was killed in a car accident. He was behind the wheel. Madison and Joshua blame him for what happened. Marcello says the kids are certain their father killed their mother."

"That's awful," Freddie said. "No wonder they came to you. They're scared and uncertain. They don't trust their own father, and from what you've told me about him, I wouldn't trust him, either."

"You haven't met him. I don't know what it is, but there is something very reassuring about Ryde. He puts you at ease, somehow."

"His kids don't seem to share that view," Freddie said. "And neither apparently do the feds."

"He was very complimentary about my performance today," Tree said.

"Soon you'll be inseparable pals," Freddie said.

"Well, the police do suspect I helped him start the fire."

"Come on," Freddie said. "They don't really—do they?"

"Markfield and Cee Jay were at my office today telling me not to leave town."

Freddie rolled her eyes. "You don't even know this guy's real name. How could you help him set a fire?"

"I do know his real name—sort of."

"So what is it?"

"Wayne Granger. He said he uses the name Ryde Bodie for business reasons."

"What kind of man does that?"

"Writers use pseudonyms all the time," Tree said.

"The kind of man who sells phony contracts to investors, the kind of man being investigated by federal authorities, who sets his house on fire, the kind of man who has a lot to hide—that's what kind of man," Freddie pronounced.

"That sounds suspiciously like you don't want me to drop this."

"Not that you would, anyway," Freddie said. "I'm sorry you didn't become an actor because maybe you wouldn't have ended up doing this. But you're doing it, and you've got yourself involved with those children, so I think you have an obligation to make sure they are safe."

As usual, Freddie was right, Tree reflected, even though he had trouble imagining Ryde, whatever his secrets and shortcomings, exposing his children to danger. He was about to say this to Freddie when his cellphone rang.

"Tree," the voice on the other end said. "This is Ryde Bodie."

"I was just thinking about you," Tree said. *And talking about you, too.*

"You see?" Ryde said with a laugh. "It's working onstage together. We're bonding."

"Is that what it is?" Tree said.

"Listen, how would you and your lovely wife like to join me for drinks and dinner Saturday night?"

Tree threw a glance at Freddie who raised her eyebrows questioningly. Tree mouthed Ryde Bodie's name.

Tree said, "Saturday night, Ryde?"

"That's right," Ryde said.

Freddie's eyebrows did a nosedive into a frown. But she nodded her head.

"Sure," Tree said. "That sounds great."

"We're going to meet at seven thirty at the place on Rabbit Road." And then, dryly: "I think you know where it is."

"I believe I can find it," Tree said.

"See you Saturday," Ryde said, and hung up.

Tree looked at Freddie. "Now you can meet the man himself."

"I can hardly wait," Freddie said, rising and stretching. "I'm beat, and I've got a long day tomorrow."

"Let's crawl into bed," Tree said. "I can tell you my life story."

"I'm all too familiar with it," Freddie said. She gave him a look. "Or am I?"

———

After Freddie went into the bedroom, Tree collected up plates and the wine glass and carried them inside. He rinsed off the plates and put them in the dishwasher along with the wine glass and then took some time washing the pan in which Freddie had broiled the turkey burgers. He was growing tired himself.

He collected the papers and magazines strewn about the TV room. He hadn't even had a chance to read the day's *News Press*. He picked it up and glanced at the front page. Just below the fold, a police mug shot of a dark-haired man with a mustache jumped out at him. The caption beneath the photo said that police had identified the body that had washed up on a Captiva Island beach earlier in the week. He was Rodrigo Ramos. According to the paper, the FBI suspected Ramos was involved with the Mexican drug cartels and was wanted on both sides of the border in connection with a number of murders.

Tree stared at the photo. He had seen this guy before. Only he wasn't dead.

That morning he had been alive and well and hosing down a yacht behind the Santini Marina Plaza.

16

"I don't want to do this," Freddie said as Tree crossed Blind Pass onto Sanibel Island, headed for dinner on Rabbit Road.

"Aren't you the least bit curious to meet him?"

"I don't like dealing with people when I'm not even certain who they are."

"Who am I? Who are any of us, really?"

"Now you're getting all existential on me."

"Seriously, I wonder who I am much of the time. God knows what anyone else is thinking."

"I'm thinking you're much more of a mystery than I anticipated."

"See? Maybe I'm not much different than Ryde Bodie."

"You have more than one name?"

Tree cast her a sidelong glance. "Maybe I'd surprise you."

"You've surprised me quite enough, thanks," Freddie said. "I don't need any more surprises."

"I know you hate these things, but try and enjoy yourself tonight."

"I'm attempting to keep an open mind."

Tree said, "That's all I ask."

"What I do for love," Freddie said as Tree's cellphone rang.

"You should not be talking into a cellphone while you're driving," Freddie said.

Tree said, "Hello?"

"Mr. C, it's me, Thomas."

Tree sighed, "Yes, Thomas. What is it?"

"That name you're looking for."

"What name?"

"You know, the body in the Traven house."

"You've got the name?"

"I do if we have a deal, Mr. C."

"Look, okay, Tommy—Thomas. Like I said, I'll do what I can."

"Well, that's still not much of a deal," Tommy said. "But I'm so proud of myself for getting the cops to give up the name, I have to tell someone."

"So who is it?"

Tree," Freddie said. "You should get off the phone."

"The dead man's name is James Edward Waterhouse."

Tree gripped the phone harder. "Jim Waterhouse? Are you sure about that?"

"You know this guy?"

"Thanks."

"Mr. C? What do you know about him?"

Tree hung up the phone.

"What was that all about?" Freddie asked.

"The body in the Traven house. It's Jim Waterhouse, the guy I encountered outside the place on Rabbit Road."

"This is the guy who said Ryde Bodie had defrauded him."

"Yes," Tree said.

"And now he's dead," Freddie said.

————

Tree turned the Mercedes into the drive on Rabbit Road. Ryde's Cadillac Escalade was parked beside a Lexus.

Freddie opened the door. Then she stopped and looked back at him. "Are you going to say anything to Ryde Bodie?"

"About what?" he said.

"Jim Waterhouse."

"No," Tree said. "For now, let's not say anything."

They came up the steps and onto the porch where they were met by Curtis, formal in a black suit and tie. Tonight, thankfully, he didn't have his AR15 Assault Rifle. He said, portentously, Tree thought, "Mr. Bodie is expecting you." Freddie gave Tree another look. He was anticipating many of those looks this evening.

Curtis led them into the sitting room dominated by a table draped in a white table cloth, laid out with stemware gleaming in candlelight. Seated nearby was a tiny Latino couple, dressed in white, matching the table cloth.

The woman turned to view the new arrivals. Her black hair was pulled into a bun away from a deep brown, hatchet-like face. The man also had black hair but his face was darker and rounder. It occurred to Tree the pair could be brother and sister—or a couple married so long they had begun to resemble one another.

Ryde rose from an easy chair, a glass of white wine in his hand. Seated on a sofa not far away dressed in a short blue flower-print dress was Bonnie, the blond woman who was Ryde's partner in the Big Arts Center Oscar show.

"There you are," Ryde said with a smile. "This must be the Fredryka Stayner I've heard so many wonderful things about."

Give Freddie her due, Tree thought, faced with a dubious evening, she could put aside her misgivings and turn on the charm full blast, which was what she did now, matching the intensity of Ryde's smile with the force of her own. The glare coming off the two of them made Tree squint.

Ryde turned to Bonnie and said, "Tree, you know Bonnie, of course. But Bonnie, I don't think you've met Freddie."

"It's a pleasure." Bonnie extended a regal hand which Freddie took.

"The three of us are doing a thing together at the Oscar show," Ryde said. "Bonnie and I were just practicing our dance moves, so I thought it might be fun if she joined us for dinner."

"Of course," Tree said. "How could anyone resist the opportunity to dine with Fred and Ginger."

Ryde turned to the tiny couple who sat very still and looked very glum. "I'd like you to meet two unexpected guests," Ryde said—a trifle uneasily, Tree thought. "Paola and Manuel are business associates from Mexico. They dropped in unexpectedly."

Manuel stood and bowed slightly before shaking Tree's hand. "Hello," he said.

The hatchet-faced woman, Paola, didn't move. She seemed content to glare at the other guests.

"I'm afraid Paola and Manuel don't speak much English," Ryde said, as if to explain the gloomy expressions on the couple's faces. He then spoke to them in Spanish. Manuel shrugged and attempted something that resembled a smile.

Ryde chuckled. Bonnie smiled brightly. So did Freddie.

Tree broke an uneasy silence by presenting Ryde with the bottle of good merlot they had brought along. Ryde passed the bottle off to the hovering Curtis and asked Freddie what she would like to drink.

"Chardonnay if you have it."

"I have a nicely oaked California white," Ryde said. "How's that?"

"That would be perfect," Freddie replied.

Ryde addressed Tree. "I know you don't drink, Tree, although I still can't get over an ex-newspaper guy *and* a detective who doesn't imbibe. Can I get you some sparkling water?"

Tree agreed that would be fine. Ryde said something in Spanish to the rigid Paola and Manuel. They both shook their heads. Ryde said to Curtis, "Apparently our Mexican guests don't want anything, Curtis. Would you mind taking care of our other guests' drinks?"

Curtis went away to get the drinks while Ryde indicated Tree and Freddie should take the loveseat. He then returned to his place on the easy chair, not far from Paola and Manuel.

"So Ryde and Bonnie, did the two of you just meet?" Freddie inquired. "Or did you know each other before the Oscar show?"

Bonnie shot Ryde a glance—a nervous glance, Tree thought.

"We've been involved in a couple of business ventures over the years," Ryde said smoothly.

"Just like Paola and Manuel," Freddie said.

"I beg your pardon?" Ryde said.

"Paola and Manuel are also business associates, too, aren't they?"

The couple, recognizing their names, adopted quizzical expressions. Paola looked at Ryde who shrugged, and said. "Yes, of course, I see what you mean."

"You might say the four of us are involved in a venture together," Bonnie said.

Ryde hastened to say, "Bonnie introduced me to the island. I was just saying how much I'm enjoying being here and how appreciative I am that she alerted me to it."

Bonnie smiled and said, "I've been coming here since I was a child."

"It really is different, isn't it?" Ryde added. "It's an undisturbed paradise compared to most of the rest of the state. I arrive on the island and immediately I am at peace."

"Even when your house burns down?" Freddie said.

Ryde's smile remained frozen in place. "These things happen in a life. I've learned to accept the good and deal with the bad. Insurance will cover most of the damages, so the way I look at it, I will come out with an even better house than before."

"Except someone ended up dead," Freddie said.

"Yes, the fellow who started the fire," Ryde replied. "I'm afraid I don't have much sympathy."

He focused on Paola and Manuel and once again spoke to them in Spanish. They did not appear to react.

"My family can remember when there wasn't the causeway," Bonnie said, changing the subject. "When Mom and Dad first came here, the only way to reach the island was by ferry. That's my first memory of the island. If you think it's unspoiled now, you should have seen it back then."

"I can imagine," Tree said.

Bonnie turned to Freddie. "What about you, Freddie? Are you a newcomer like Ryde?"

"A bit of an interloper, I'm afraid," Freddie said. "But like you, Tree used to come here as a boy."

Tree nodded. "Every winter for a couple of weeks."

"Then you know what it was like," Bonnie said.

"We were pretty easy to please back then," Tree said. "Put us on the beach looking for seashells or throw us into the ocean, and we were happy."

"Do you still go shelling?" Ryde asked.

Tree shook his head. "I can't even remember the last time I swam in the ocean."

"I swam in the ocean this morning," Bonnie said.

"Bonnie's a former dancer," Ryde said, as if that explained swimming in the ocean.

"A long time ago," Bonnie said.

"Before you and Ryde were involved in business together?"

"Long before." Bonnie smiled sweetly.

"That's why she moves so well on stage," Ryde said. "She is such a pleasure to dance with."

"Where did you dance?" Freddie inquired.

"Vegas mostly," Bonnie said. "A little bit in Atlantic City. But mostly Vegas."

Ryde said, "Robert Goulet once asked her out."

"And then stood me up," Bonnie said ruefully. "Not much of a claim to fame. I was just a kid. Eighteen. Lying about my age."

Paola and Manuel both jumped as Curtis reentered with the drinks. Ryde helped him distribute them. Once everyone had settled again, Freddie looked at Ryde and said, "What about your children, Mr. Bodie? I understand you have a boy and a girl. How do they like it here?"

"They're settling in." Ryde cast a glance at Paola and Manuel before he continued smoothly: "It's a big change for them, but Madison likes her school. Joshua's a little more problematic, but he's going to be okay. He just needs more time to get used to things changing."

"It's too bad they're not here tonight," Freddie said. "I'd like to meet them."

Ryde looked past Freddie and said to the hovering Curtis, "How are we coming with dinner?"

"Almost ready, Mr. Bodie," Curtis reported. "Maybe everyone would like to get seated."

"You heard the man," Ryde said, bouncing to his feet. "It looks like dinner is served."

As they walked toward the table, Ryde clapped Tree on the back, and said, "It's good to see you, Tree. Glad you could make it—so I could meet your beautiful wife."

Freddie said, "The wife who didn't get her question answered."

Ryde's face went blank. "What's that?"

"About your children."

He broke into another smile. "Right. The kids. They're at a sleepover at a friend's house."

"How wonderful that they've managed to make friends so fast," Freddie said.

"Isn't it?" Ryde held a chair for Freddie. "Why don't you sit here beside me? I'm fascinated by the supermarket business."

Tree held Bonnie's chair so that she was seated beside him. Curtis entered and poured more wine. Ryde aimed a grin around the table at his guests once Curtis departed. "Isn't this great?" he said. "Having you all here like this." He raised his glass. "Cheers everyone. To many happy Sanibel sunsets."

"Happy sunsets," said Bonnie.

Everyone clinked glasses. Everyone that is except Paola and Manuel. They sat stiffly, glowering at the other guests.

Curtis appeared from the kitchen carrying a tureen of soup. As he approached the table, Ryde began to frown. "Curtis," he said. "What's this? I thought we agreed we weren't going to serve soup tonight."

For a moment, Tree thought the man who appeared in the doorway was a late-arriving guest, and wondered who this guy was who would turn up in black leather wearing a motorcycle helmet.

Then Curtis dropped the soup tureen. It smashed to the floor. Tree followed the descent of the tureen, so it was a moment before he noticed the newcomer was pointing the ugly snout of what appeared to be a sawed-off shotgun.

Ryde started to his feet, his mouth opening to say something, when the black-clad intruder pulled the trigger. The blast blew a hole in Curtis's chest, spraying blood, and sending him staggering back. Beside him, Bonnie began to scream. The hatchet-faced woman was on her feet as the intruder raised the shotgun again. Without thinking, Tree lurched forward and grabbed at the weapon, knocking against the intruder. He slipped on the soup-covered floor as he fired a second time. Ryde cried out and fell back.

The shotgun spun out of the intruder's hands, landing on the table. Manuel raised a knife and plunged it deep into the intruder's chest. The intruder cried out, turned, and again slipped, crashing to the floor.

The hatchet-faced woman snarled something unintelligible before she hurried from the room. Manuel looked at Tree and then, still holding the knife, disappeared, as if the unfolding drama had been played out on a stage, and he had dropped through a trap door in the floor.

Tree spun around, searching for Freddie. A fine mist seemed to have descended in the room. Through the mist, Tree could hear Bonnie screaming. Real horror movie screams. Freddie was not joining in, however. She was too busy holding Ryde Bodie in her arms.

17

Detectives Cee Jay Boone and Owen Markfield showed up to investigate the shooting and stabbing on Rabbit Road. Curtis, the bodyguard, was pronounced dead at the scene, as was the black-clad gunman in the motorcycle helmet. Ryde, suffering a gunshot wound to the shoulder, had been rushed to Lee Memorial Hospital and was now in the intensive care unit. Bonnie also was taken to the hospital suffering shock.

Markfield kept looking at Tree and shaking his head, as if he could not believe Tree was at the scene of yet another dead body. Freddie said she did not want to stay in the house now filling with crime scene investigators, everyone stepping gingerly around a floor covered with an unsightly mixture of soup and blood.

Markfield and Cee Jay escorted Tree and Freddie outside. The Florida night was warm and pleasant. The driveway was jammed with police and emergency vehicles. Officers had set up crime scene LED lights on tripods, lighting the outside of the house like a movie set, which in a macabre way, it was. Someone had set lawn chairs in the backyard.

Tree let Freddie do most of the talking, since her recollection of events was clear and concise as opposed to his, shrouded in blurry movement through a shifting fog: the arrival of the intruder in the motorcycle helmet with a shotgun; the hatchet-faced woman frozen in place; Manuel raising a knife; everything moving too quickly. Freddie was able to bring focus and form to all of it.

Tree slamming into the gunman was made to seem like an act of selfless courage rather than the unthinking action of a guy who an hour after the event could barely remember what he had done. Markfield shook his head again and then focused on Tree with a look that might have been mistaken for grudging respect.

"So, after you knocked the gun out of this guy's hand, tell me again what happened," Markfield said.

"Then Manuel stabbed him with a knife," Tree said.

"And then he and this woman named Paola, they took off?"

"That's right."

"Why would they run away?"

"I have no idea," Tree said.

"Ryde said they were business associates from Mexico," Freddie said.

Markfield shot Cee Jay a look before again focusing on Tree.

"So as a result of this Oscar show, Ryde Bodie invited you here tonight. Is that what happened?"

"He invited us for dinner," Tree explained patiently. "Bonnie was also present when we arrived. She and Ryde are supposed to dance together."

Markfield made more notes. "And there was no other reason for the dinner?"

"Not as far as I know," Tree said.

"No business discussed?"

"What kind of business would we discuss?"

"I don't know," Markfield said. "These two Mexicans are business associates, apparently. And you are working for Bodie, are you not?"

"Yes, I suppose I am," Tree said. "But that wasn't discussed."

"This is the guy who owns the house on Captiva Drive that recently burned to the ground," Markfield pointed out.

"What? You think we all sat around talking about setting more fires around the island?"

Markfield didn't respond. Instead, he busied himself writing in his notebook. When he lifted his head again, he said, "Why do you suppose anyone would want to shoot Ryde Bodie?"

"I don't know," Tree said. "I have no idea. At first I thought the guy was a guest."

"A guest in a motorcycle helmet," Markfield said.

"I wondered about that," Tree said.

Cee Jay: "You don't know if Mr. Bodie had any enemies?"

"Other than the guy who tried to kill him tonight, no," Tree said. "Do you have any idea who he is?"

"He wasn't carrying any identification," Cee Jay said. "He's a kid in his twenties, Latino. He was using a sawed off twelve gauge shotgun, a Super-Shorty, it's called. Very compact. Easily hidden. We found a Kawasaki Ninja outside that he must have rode in on. You're sure you don't know anyone who might have a grudge against Bodie?"

Tree said, "You probably know more about why someone would want to shoot him than I do."

Cee Jay did not say anything.

"Here's the thing you should be concerned about," Freddie interjected. "Ryde has young children, a son and a daughter. Someone should find out where they are, make sure they're okay, and let them know that their father is in hospital."

"Any idea where they might be?" Cee Jay addressed Freddie.

"Ryde said something about a sleepover, but he didn't say where."

"That doesn't give us much to go on," Markfield said.

"But we'll see what we can do." Cee Jay, reassuring.

———————

On the way home after the police finally released them, Freddie tucked her hand under Tree's arm and laid her head on his shoulder and said, "That was pretty amazing what you did back there."

"You think so?"

"First of all, you probably saved Ryde's life by jumping that guy. Maybe our lives, too. After he finished with Curtis and Ryde, he probably would have let us have it."

"Let us have it?"

"Isn't that what they say?"

"Only in old gangster movies."

"Everyone else was panicking and ducking for cover, but somehow you kept your head about you. Like Harrison Ford in *Patriot Games*."

"Harrison Ford in *Patriot Games*?"

"You know, those Irish terrorists are about to assassinate members of the Royal Family in broad daylight. Harrison doesn't run away from trouble, he runs towards it and saves the day."

"I'm your Harrison Ford," Tree said.

"You're better than Harrison Ford," Freddie said.

"Except I can barely remember doing any of the things you just said I did."

"The point is you did them."

But it was a blur. All of it. A blur.

18

"That's the word they used on the radio," Todd Jackson was saying Monday morning when he arrived for coffee with Tree and Rex at the Visitors Center.

Rex put his coffee down on Tree's desk and said, "Hero? They actually said that?"

"It was right there on the radio," Todd said. "I practically drove off the road."

"You shouldn't be operating heavy machinery at a moment like that," Rex said.

"So Tree," Todd said. "How does it feel to be a *heee-ro?*"

"Come on, give me a break you guys," Tree said from behind his desk. He'd almost not come in that morning, but Freddie was up as usual and on her way into Dayton's—nothing, not even a Saturday night dinner party shooting, would stop her going to work. So Tree had trundled down to the Visitors Center, only to spend the morning deflecting calls from local media outlets anxious for comments from "the hero" who had "prevented a worse tragedy" after a "Sanibel Island dinner party erupted in violence, leaving one man dead and another in critical condition in Lee Memorial Hospital."

"This is the part where you say, 'I'm no hero,'" Rex said.

"I'm no hero," Tree said.

"I think you're crazy," Rex said.

"Much more likely than me being a hero."

"I see it as part of your ongoing campaign to single-handedly destroy tourism on the island," Rex said.

"So give us the blow by blow," Todd said. "Tell us exactly what happened."

"Interestingly enough, I don't remember much," Tree said. "I heard the shotgun blast, and I remember seeing this fellow Curtis blown back."

"One heck of a mess at that range," Todd interjected.

"And I remember worrying about Freddie, thinking that I had to get to her. Otherwise, though, it's all pretty much a blur, until the police arrived."

"Thank goodness," Todd said. "Otherwise, Tree would get a big head, and he'd be impossible to live with."

"He's impossible to live with now," Rex said.

The telephone rang. Tree looked at the readout and didn't recognize the number. It could be another reporter. Or—just maybe—a potential client. He was still in business, after all. He picked up the receiver and said, "Sanibel Sunset Detective. Tree Callister speaking."

For a moment there was silence on the other end of the line, and then: "Hey, buddy. How are you doing?"

"Ryde?" Tree could hardly believe it was him on the line.

"Look, I'm sorry about the ruckus the other night. Are you okay? What about Freddie?"

"I'm all right. I'm surprised you're able to make a phone call."

"Thanks to you most of the blast missed me," Ryde said. "They got me out of intensive care about an hour ago."

"I'm glad to hear it," Tree said. "You had me worried. I wasn't sure you were going to make it."

"Oh, I'm going to make it," Ryde said. "But I feel badly for Freddie. Please apologize to her for me. I hope she's okay."

"She'll be glad to hear you're going to be okay," Tree said. "Have you talked to the police?"

"No, the doctors wouldn't let them near me, but it's a matter of time before they come back. In the meantime, Tree, I need you over here."

"What do you need me for?"

"Security. I'm all alone here. What with Curtis gone, I don't have anyone to keep an eye on things. So as of now, Tree, I'm hiring you—or rehiring you, I guess."

"I don't know that I'd be much good to you as a bodyguard, Ryde."

"You already saved my life once. That's a pretty good start."

"Whatever happened or didn't happen was more a case of blind luck than anything to do with my abilities as a bodyguard."

"Look, I'm still alive today, and you're the reason why. Now, please, get over here. I've got no one else I can turn to."

———————

The four stories of Lee Memorial were built around an impressive atrium. A piano player kept things calm in the main reception area, giving the visitor an unexpected feeling of peace. The tinkling sound of a piano in the atrium and all was right with the world.

Except for the odd patient with a bullet in him, Tree reflected as he stepped on the elevator to the third floor.

He found Ryde in a private room, lying on his back sound asleep, pale and unshaven, hooked up to a breathing tube, an intravenous drip, and a catheter snaking out from under his bed covers.

Ryde came awake slowly as Tree seated himself beside the bed. He struggled to produce a weak smile, nowhere near his usual incandescence. "Hey, buddy," he said. "Glad you're here."

"Ryde, you don't look good," Tree said.

"I'm okay," he said. "Looks worse than it is. Isn't that what everyone says?"

"Only in bad movies."

"Hey, life is a bad movie," Ryde said. "I just hope Freddie's okay."

"She's fine," Tree said.

"Wonderful woman. A beauty. You're a very fortunate man, Tree. She's something else. That's my big regret about all this, that Freddie and I didn't have a chance to get to know each other better. Such a shame. Spoiled a great evening."

"Spoiled a great evening? Ryde, a man is dead. You're shot. And your kids, what about them? Are they okay?"

"The kids are fine." Ryde closed his eyes, and for a moment Tree wondered if he hadn't drifted off. Then they opened again and he murmured, "Poor Curtis. I'm afraid he didn't do much of a job protecting me. You'd think at the least he would have made sure the front door was locked." He winked at Tree. "Good thing I had my secret security guard there, right, buddy?"

"Do you know who tried to kill you?"

"Isn't that the damnedest thing? Can you believe what happened?"

"No, I can't, Ryde. One moment Curtis is starting to serve soup. The next moment there's a guy in a motorcycle helmet blasting away with a sawed-off shotgun."

"I told him specifically I didn't want a soup course. This is Florida. It's too hot. We talked about it in the afternoon. He knew I didn't want soup. Can you believe that?"

"You know Manuel stabbed the intruder?"

"He's a tough little guy that Manuel, I wouldn't mess with him. Paola, too."

"What happened to them? Why did they run away like that?"

"The thing is, Tree—and please tell Freddie this—you don't have to worry about Joshua and Madison. They are safe. Wonderful kids. I'm glad they didn't see their old man shot like that. No, no. Just as well they weren't there. Neither one of them likes soup, anyway."

"Where are they, Ryde?"

"Safe. Not to worry about them. Right now, we got bigger problems to deal with."

"What problems do we have, Ryde?"

"I wonder what kind of soup Curtis made," Ryde said. "You tell him not to make soup, and then he goes ahead and makes it. Now he's dead. How do you like that? What kind of soup was it?"

"Ryde?"

"I mean, I don't even like soup all that much. And what's so good about soup that, despite everything, you go ahead and make it, anyway? Maybe we can find out, Tree. Do you suppose we can?"

"Ryde, where are the kids?" Tree demanded.

Instead of answering, Ryde produced a faint smile and settled back against the pillows. He closed his eyes.

"Ryde?" Tree said.

The wounded man began to breathe softly, asleep again.

———

Every so often Ryde shifted in the bed, producing a snore, but otherwise he remained fast asleep. A pretty young nurse entered the room. She checked the plasma bag and then did something with the LCD screen monitoring Ryde's heart and blood pressure.

Tree introduced himself. The young nurse said her name was Lindsay. She asked if Tree was a relative. Tree said he was in charge of Mr. Bodie's security. Nurse Lindsay looked at him curiously and then said Ryde was the first patient she'd had requiring security. "You don't have a gun or anything like that, do you?"

"I provide security without a gun," Tree said.

"That's good," Nurse Lindsay said. "Guns make me very nervous."

"Me, too," Tree said.

Nurse Lindsay said, "I don't mean any offense, but aren't you a little old to be doing this sort of thing?"

"You mean sitting here?"

"Providing security. What if something should happen?"

"I sit here hoping nothing will happen," Tree said.

Nurse Lindsay gave him one more dubious look before exiting with a crisp swish of starched efficiency.

About five o'clock, Tree grew tired of being a bodyguard and decided to stretch his legs. There was no sign of Lindsay, but another nurse directed him to the cafeteria. He shared the elevator with an old man on a gurney, attended to by a hulking male nurse in green hospital scrubs. "This would be a great place if it wasn't for the sick people," the old man said to the hulking nurse. The nurse just stared at him. The old man looked at Tree. "What do you think?" he asked.

"It gives the place charm," Tree said.

"Maybe you're right," the old man said.

Tree bought a smoothie in the cafeteria. He saw Nurse Lindsay sitting with three or four other nurses and a couple of young doctors in white hospital coats. He waved at her. She looked at him and gave a vague wave back. He was leaving the cafeteria when his cellphone rang. Freddie said, "Hi. Where are you?"

"I'm at the hospital with Ryde Bodie."

"What are you doing there?"

"I'm providing security," Tree said.

"For Ryde?"

"That's right." Did he sound defensive when he said this?

"Shouldn't the police be doing that?"

"Well, they're not."

"Listen to me, my love. You almost got yourself killed. If someone comes for him again, what in the world could you ever do, except maybe end up dead this time?"

"You're the second person in the last few minutes to question my ability to protect a client."

"This is something for the police," Freddie said.

"There are no police, there's only me," Tree said. "I may not be much, but right now, I'm all he's got."

"I know I waste my breath when I say this, but please, be careful."

"Call me Careful Callister," Tree said.

"That'll be the day," Freddie replied, and hung up.

Tree took the elevator back up to Ryde's room. By now it was approaching six o'clock. Metal dinner carts were being rolled out along the corridor, filling the air with the warm, neutral aroma that bland hospital food gives off.

Tree stepped back into Ryde's room. Except Ryde was no longer there.

19

Freddie was surprised to see Tree when he arrived home. "I thought Careful Callister was providing security," she said.

"It's difficult to provide security for someone who's not there."

"What does that mean?"

"It means that Ryde is no longer at Lee County Memorial."

"How can that be? He was shot."

"Apparently a little thing like a gunshot wound doesn't stop Ryde Bodie."

"Do you have any idea where he went?"

"Who knows?" Tree said. "Certainly I don't."

"If I didn't know any better," Freddie said, "I would say the Sanibel Sunset Detective is somewhat upset."

"I don't get this guy," Tree said. "I truly don't."

Nurse Lindsay had not seen Ryde leave, and neither had anyone else on the floor. Somehow, either by himself or with someone's help, he had disentangled himself from the monitor, pulled out the IV drip, not to mention his catheter, dressed, and left.

"He couldn't keep his eyes open while I was there," Tree said. "In fact, he slept the entire afternoon."

"Until you left," Freddie said.

"I just went downstairs to stretch my legs and get something to drink."

"So maybe he wasn't really asleep."

"But he has a bullet hole in him," Tree said. "I can't believe he just left the hospital."

Freddie said, "Why would he hire you to protect him and then leave?"

Tree was saved from having to answer a question for which he had no answer, by his ringing telephone. "I should take this," he said to Freddie. "It may be Ryde."

But it wasn't. "Hey, Mr. C," Tommy Dobbs said.

"Tommy, I can't talk right now," Tree said, trying to keep the note of irritation out of his voice. Not trying very hard.

"I've been thinking all day about what to do, Mr. Callister. So before I do anything, I really think it's important we talk."

"It'll have to wait."

"I think we'd better do this tonight, Mr. C. Otherwise, it may be too late."

"Where are you?"

"I'm outside your house."

Tree closed his eyes momentarily, and then said, "All right. Stay there. I'll be right out."

He looked at Freddie. "It's Tommy Dobbs."

She looked at him expectantly.

"He's outside. He wants to talk to me."

"Well, okay," Freddie said. "You'd better invite him in."

Tree thought of Tommy going on about nine million dollars and a story in *The Chicago Sun-Times*. Right now, he did not need those complications. "It'll be a lot faster if I just talk to him outside."

"I'm never quite sure exactly what you're up to."

"That makes two of us," Tree said.

A banged up Chevy Impala, with Tommy huddled behind the wheel, was parked on the roadside. Tree wondered if he looked as dumb and out of place as Tommy did when he was staking out someone. Probably.

The passenger door opened with a grinding howl as Tree slid in beside Tommy. "This had better be good," Tree said.

"This is good, Mr. Callister," Tommy said. "Believe me, you won't be disappointed."

The sartorially resplendent Thomas Dobbs had disappeared—possibly with the confession he wasn't yet part of the *Sun-Times* editorial staff— replaced by a more island-friendly character wearing knee-length New Balance workout shorts, a Florida Gators T-shirt, and a New York Yankees baseball cap.

He shifted around in his seat so that he faced Tree. His face in the uncertain street light was flushed with excitement. "Like I said to you earlier, I've been trying to decide all day what to do. Whether to come to you or to go to the police. Finally, I decided I should meet with you, see what you think, and go from there."

"I have no idea what you're talking about."

"What I'm talking about is where I was the other night. And what I saw. That's what I'm talking about."

"Where were you?"

"Let's put it this way. I was at a certain address on Rabbit Road."

Even in the darkness, Tree could see the flush of excitement on Tommy's face. "You were outside Ryde Bodie's house?"

"Let's say for the sake of argument I was."

"What were you doing out there?"

"What else? Following you, Mr. C."

"Tommy, how many times have I asked you not to follow me around?"

"I know, but maybe this time it's just as well I didn't listen to you. I was sitting there trying to stay awake, when I heard this loud blast and then, shortly after that, a second loud blast. The next thing I know, this little man and woman run from the house."

"Okay. Then what?"

"I wasn't sure what had happened. They got into a van parked at the side of the house. I hadn't noticed it before. I figured something was wrong, and so I followed them."

"You followed the van?"

"That's right."

"Where did it go?"

"That's the thing, Mr. C. The police are looking for these people, right?"

"Yes, they are," Tree said.

"I can take you to them."

"Tommy, we don't do this. You go to the police."

"If that's all I wanted, I would have gone to the cops already. No, Mr. C, there's a big story here, and together we can make it happen. Tree Callister, the Sanibel Sunset Detective, solves the mystery of the Rabbit Road Shootout—aided by his pal, ace Chicago reporter Thomas Dobbs."

"You've got to stop looking at me like I'm some sort of ticket to the top of your imaginary journalistic mountain. I'm not."

The excitement had faded from Tommy's face, replaced by a petulance Tree had not seen before. "Do you want to see where these people went, or not?"

Tree sighed and said, "How far away are we talking about?"

"Not too far. At least have a look. Then if you decide we need the cops, well, okay. I'll go along with that. How's that for a deal?"

"I'm not trying to make a deal with you."

"Don't tell me you're not curious. I'll bet the last thing in the world you expected was this guy Bodie getting shot. I'll bet you're trying to figure it out. You're not telling the police much, I know that. They think you're withholding information. There's more going on here than meets the eye, I'll bet you anything. So what do you say, Mr. C? You want to go for a ride or not?"

20

Elvis sang "Viva Las Vegas," as Tommy Dobbs turned onto I-75 headed south toward Naples.

"Turn that down, will you?" Tree said as he poked out a number on his cellphone.

Freddie answered almost immediately. "Where are you?" Trying not to sound angry.

"I'm with Tommy. We're headed south on I-75, but don't ask me where we're going."

"Tree, how could you just take off like that? I've been worried."

"It's the only way he would do this," Tree said.

"Tell her I'm sorry," Tommy said, eyes on the road ahead.

"Did you hear that?"

"What?" Freddie demanded.

"Tommy says he's sorry."

"Tree, this has nothing to do with anyone else's crazy. It has to do with your crazy. You're the one I worry about."

"At times like this, I worry too."

"But you still go off and do these things."

"I know," Tree said. "But then I don't know."

"I've got to go," Freddie said. "It's late and I have to be up first thing in the morning."

"I'll stay in touch."

Freddie hung up the phone.

Tree swallowed a couple of times, trying to keep the anger in the pit of his stomach where he could control it. He wasn't so much angry at Tommy, who, he had to admit, was only trying to help. No, he was furious with himself. He had a beautiful, wonderful wife who loved him waiting at a comfortable home where there was not a care in the world. What the hell was he doing to himself—not to mention what he might be doing to his marriage?

There was no answer. Only the madness of Tree Callister.

"This had better be good," Tree repeated, this time through gritted teeth.

"Don't you think Elvis remains the great mystery of American popular culture, Mr. C?"

"I don't care," Tree said. "Let's just get this over with."

"Here was a young guy from the South, a truck driver, a polite, intelligent teenager who came from a good home full of strong values. He wasn't a rebel in any real sense of the word, hadn't even really performed in public before he walked into Sun records. Yet somehow he was able to create this ground-breaking music, unlike anything anyone had heard before. Then he threw it all away, made thirty lousy movies because a bunch of old guys thought that was the right thing to do. And even though he probably knew better, he allowed himself to become addicted to prescription drugs, ended up having a heart attack, and falling off a toilet. This totally unique talent self-destructed and died at the age of forty-two. There's something awesomely, tragically American about that, don't you think?"

"This is not a subject I'm currently giving a whole lot of thought to," Tree said.

"How did that happen? You've got everything in the world you could ever want, and you throw it all away."

Yes, you do, Tree thought. Yes, you do.

"Why do we chase after the sort of fame and fortune Elvis attained?" Tommy rattled on. "What do we think? That somehow it's going to make us happy? If you look at

Elvis and Michael Jackson, Janis Joplin, Whitney Houston, the list goes on and on, reaching the top didn't make any of them happy. Just the opposite in fact. It destroyed them."

"That's why I want to be Mick Jagger in the next life," Tree said. "He seemed to get through just fine—and he's still out there, dancing."

"Just like you, Mr. Callister," Tommy said, taking his eyes off the road momentarily and throwing Tree a sly grin. "You're still out there dancing."

"If I end up dancing alone, thanks to you and your hare-brained ideas, I'm going to kill you. I swear I will."

———

Two hours later, Tree was fighting to stay awake when Tommy swung the Chevy Impala off Tamiami Trail East onto Collier Avenue. He drove past the sign that marked the entrance to Everglades City. They had arrived on the southwestern edge of Everglades National Park. Tree couldn't believe it. "You followed them here?"

"That's something, isn't it? Pretty amazing, don't you think?"

Tree didn't say anything, but he thought: two idiots on a wild goose chase driving into Everglades City in the middle of the night. Insane.

Along Collier Avenue, the Chevy's headlights caught tall palm trees staked out on the median. A motel flashed by on the right. They passed silent one-story houses, their driveways choked with pickup trucks and power boats perched atop trailers.

Tommy turned onto a side street that soon exhausted any pretense of being a road and became a dirt track threaded through bursts of mangrove. Cypress trees pushed against the track. Beyond the mangrove, some-where in the darkness, if Tree had his geography right, Chokoloskee Bay, its Ten Thousand Islands, and the Gulf of Mexico.

Tommy turned into a narrow clearing and brought the Chevy to a stop. Tree stared out the windshield at—what? There was nothing to see. At least nothing Tree could see.

"Yeah, this is the place," Tommy decided, reassuring himself as much as Tree. "Come on."

They got out of the car, Tree stretching, his sciatic nerve sending shards of pain pulsing down cramped legs. He limped along, deciding he was getting too old for these long rides. He was getting too old for everything, certainly for an early morning wild goose chase like this. He felt tired and stupid, and the sight of Tommy peering into the distance annoyed him even more.

"What's the matter now?"

"I think we're in the right place," Tommy said. "It was so dark that night, it's hard to say . . ." His voice trailed off.

"Hard to say what?" Tree demanded. "Come on, enough's enough. What are we doing here?"

Instead of answering, Tommy stalked away, headed back to the roadway. Tree called after him. Tommy turned and put a finger to his lips, demanding quiet. Tree rolled his eyes, and then followed him.

The track took a sharp left, past a cypress tree draped in moss partially obscuring the view of a cabin on stilts above a rickety dock. A sleek ivory yacht was tied to the dock. Tree realized with a start this was *el Trueno*, the same craft he had seen moored at the marina in Fort Myers Beach.

"This is the place they ended up at after the shooting," Tommy whispered. "This is where I followed them."

"Was the boat here?" Tree asked.

Tommy nodded. "Yes, it was."

"What did they do when they got here?"

"The two of them went inside. Then, about an hour later a couple of guys showed up in an SUV, and went inside."

"Then what?"

"Then I got the hell out of there," Tommy said.

No one appeared to be moving inside the cabin. The boat also looked deserted.

"I don't think anyone's there now," Tree said.

"Let's take a look." And before Tree could think about stopping him, Tommy crouched, and then began running like a wobbly stork toward the shack. Tree started after him. Tommy mounted the narrow porch framing the rear of the shack. By the time Tree clambered up the steps, Tommy was peering in the window of the back door. "It's locked," he announced.

No sooner had he said that than the door opened. The tiny, hatchet-faced woman Ryde called Paola stood there holding a gun. She cried something loud and angry in Spanish an instant before Tommy, in a quick thinking act that astonished Tree, smashed her in the jaw with his fist. The woman flew back, dropping the gun as she took flight. She landed inside the cabin, her head striking the floorboards with a loud crack.

Tommy crashed into the interior, Tree following. The woman lay on her back, not moving, the gun a few feet away. Tree knelt down to her. Tommy, meanwhile, was bent over, holding his fighting hand, and moaning. Tree glanced at him. "What's the matter with you?"

"I think I broke my hand," Tommy said. "Is she dead?"

She certainly wasn't moving. How do you find a pulse? Tree tried to remember what he'd read about it. Use two fingers. Okay. Press in the hollow between the wind pipe and the large muscle in the neck. He did that. No pulse. He couldn't feel a pulse. They had killed tiny, gun-toting Paola. Holding his two fingers together, he pressed harder into the hollow of the woman's neck, and—thanks to whatever gods control these things— got a pulse.

"She's alive," Tree said.

He heard Tommy exhale loudly. But then he became tense again. "Suppose she's in some sort of coma? Suppose she never wakes up again."

A door across the room opened, a light went on, and a tiny head poked into view. "She's dead," Madison announced loudly. "The wicked witch is dead!"

21

Joshua appeared a moment later, squeezing past Madison for a better look at the woman on the floor. He then looked anxiously at Tree. "You didn't kill her, did you?"

"No, I didn't. Are the two of you okay?"

"You know these kids?" Tommy said in a surprised voice. He was still holding his hand.

"Of course he knows us," Madison said. "He's *working* for us."

Tommy looked at Tree. "These kids hired you?"

"It's a long story," Tree said, straightening to inspect the children. They appeared to be in good shape.

Madison pointed at the woman and said, "I don't like her, she's mean."

"Worse, she's a lousy cook," Joshua said.

"How did you get here?" Tree asked.

"They brought us on a boat," Madison said.

"Do you know why they took you away?"

"They told us Dad was in trouble and we had to go with them until everything was safe again," Joshua explained. "Only when we got here, Madison and I began to think these people were lying to us."

"They *were* lying to us," Madison declared. "I warned them, I said you were working for us, and that you would come to get us, and sure enough, I was right."

"*We* were right," Joshua corrected.

"I gotta get to a doctor," Tommy said. "My hand is killing me."

Behind them, the hatchet-faced Paola suddenly sprang to her feet. Tree couldn't believe her speed. Almost as fast, her hand shot into Tommy's crotch. He howled with a combination of terror and pain, flailing uselessly at the woman, who hung onto him for dear life. Madison started to cry and Joshua's face twisted into a look of anguish.

Tree saw the gun on the floor, snatched it up, marched over to where Tommy and the woman grappled together and clipped the gun across her head.

Paola grunted, and loosened her grip on Tommy. Blood streamed down her forehead as she swung around to Tree. Small black pinpoint eyes burned with hatred. She opened her mouth and literally snarled.

He pointed the gun at her, holding it at arm's length. "Stay right there," he ordered in his most authoritative voice—a voice that, to his ears, did not sound all that authoritative. She poised on the points of her feet, body tensed, ready to pounce, that hatchet face sternly set. Then she issued what could only be described as a cackle—it occurred to Tree that maybe the kids were right about the witch part—and then she was gone.

By the time Tree decided he couldn't shoot her, she was out the door. He raced onto the porch as Paola reached the bottom of the stairs. He thought again about shooting at her, but she had already disappeared into the darkness of the encroaching mango and cypress trees.

He stepped back into the cabin. Joshua and Madison were crying. Tommy was down on his knees, holding his crotch.

"Tommy, are you okay?"

"I'm fine, I'm fine," Tommy said. "Just give me a minute."

Tree went to the kids. "It's all right," he said, trying to make his quavering voice sound reassuring. "It's going to be all right. Thanks to my friend, Tommy, you're safe now."

"It's *not* safe," Madison wailed. "She's a witch. She's going to come back for us."

"She's not a witch, Madison," Tree said in a calming voice.

Madison wasn't having any of it. "Yes, she is," she cried. "Even they call her a witch behind her back."

"You keep saying 'they,' was there someone else other than the witch?"

Madison nodded. "There were three of them, including the black-haired man, who was just as bad as the witch."

"But the little man was all right," Joshua interjected. "He kept telling us we would be okay—in English. The others, they all spoke in these foreign languages," Joshua said.

"They didn't speak in foreign languages," Madison corrected disdainfully. "They spoke *Spanish*."

"That's a foreign language, Joshua insisted.

"It can't be that foreign," Madison countered. "Daddy speaks it."

Tree helped Tommy to his feet. "Did you see what she did to me?" he moaned. "She ruined my junk, that's what she did. I'm ruined for life."

"What's junk?" Madison asked.

Joshua made a face at her. "Madison, you don't know *anything*."

Tree herded everyone outside, Tommy leaning on him as they moved along the roadway back to the Chevy. Tree got the kids strapped into seatbelts in the back and then helped Tommy ease himself into the front passenger seat amid a chorus of grunts and groans.

Tree got behind the wheel and started up the Chevy, half expecting the witch to fly out from the underbrush and throw herself against the car's windshield, as in one of the horror movies that age had made it impossible for him to watch. There were enough real life horrors, thanks very much, without paying to see them on a movie screen.

As Tree backed out onto the roadway and started back for Everglades City, Elvis was on the radio singing "Rock-a-Hula Baby."

Madison called out from the back seat. "What's that awful music?"

For a long time on the way back to Fort Myers, Tree imagined an SUV or a pickup truck roaring up behind them, Paola, the witch of Everglades City, in full pursuit. But as the Chevy swept past Naples, Tree began to relax: no one was coming after them. By this time, the children were fast asleep in the back, and even the ever-complaining Tommy had subsided into a sullen, exhausted silence, holding his fight-damaged hand, leaning his head against the side window.

The question nagging at Tree: what was Paola doing with Ryde's son and daughter? The kids themselves seemed to have no clue, other than to fuel their already ingrained suspicion that something wasn't right with their father—wherever he was.

More pressing was the issue of what to do with the kids. Go to the police? That would be Freddie's solution—that was always Freddie's solution. But for the moment,

Tree decided, that wasn't the answer. Detective Owen Markfield was no friend and right now he needed friends.

What with the traffic and the necessity to fill up the gas tank and the kids wanting to stop for something to eat, it was late morning by the time Tree crossed the causeway onto Sanibel Island. He telephoned Freddie.

"Are you all right?" She sounded anxious.

"Yes, I'm fine," Tree said. "I've got Ryde Bodie's kids with me."

"Where did you find them?"

"In Everglades City. I'm going to take them to the house. Tommy, too. He's hurt his hand."

"What were they doing there?"

"I'm not sure. They were with Paola, the woman who was at Ryde's place."

"What did you do about her?"

"After Tommy punched her and I hit her with a gun, she ran away."

Dead silence while Freddie processed this information. "All right," she said slowly. "You think it's a good idea to bring the kids to our place?"

"I'm not sure what's going on, so until I can get to the bottom of it, I don't want to let them out of my sight."

"Look, I'm in the middle of back-to-back meetings, but I'll get away as soon as I can and come home."

"I think we're okay for now," Tree said.

The silence at the other end of the line rang in his ear.

———————

Once they arrived at the house and he had everyone settled—the kids said they weren't tired, and then fell asleep as soon as they lay down; Tommy stretched out on the sofa and immediately began snoring—Tree went back out to the Beetle and drove over to the Sanibel School. Fighting to stay awake, he once again joined the Parent Pickup line. Presently, a bell rang signaling the return of the student population to its parents.

Marcello made his appearance, sauntering out, surrounded by his usual entourage. However, this time Marcello's face didn't light up when he saw Tree. "I've been trying to get hold of you," he said.

"I've got Madison and Joshua," Tree said.

Marcello looked surprised. "You do? Where'd you find them?"

"In Everglades City."

"That's some detective work." Marcello actually sounded impressed. "Where are they now?"

"They're at my house for the time being. Listen, I need your help."

"You do?" As if he couldn't believe it.

"Can you come to my place?"

Marcello gave him a sideways look. "That mean we're partners?"

Tree sighed deeply. "All right, yes. For the moment, we're partners."

That got a smile from Marcello—a hint of triumph in the smile. "Thing is, you gotta call Mrs. Lake and let her know I'm staying with you."

Tree telephoned the boy's foster mother on the way back to Andy Rosse Lane. "A sleepover?" Mrs. Lake, as usual, sounded dubious.

"Freddie and I are babysitting a couple of Marcello's classmates, so we thought it might be a good idea if Marcello could stay with them and help Freddie and I babysit."

"You're not giving me much warning," said Mrs. Lake.

"Sorry, this just came up," Tree said. "Look, if it's a problem, I'll just drive Marcello home."

"No, no, if that's what he wants, it's fine with me." She paused and then said, "Providing it doesn't have anything to do with Marcello being a private detective or anything silly like that."

"No," said Tree, not very convincingly.

Marcello was beaming as Tree ended the phone call. "The two Sanibel Sunset detectives," he pronounced with glee.

Tree groaned.

Freddie was home by the time he arrived with Marcello. She had Tommy holding an ice pack wrapped in a towel against his swelling hand. She had engineered a bath for Madison and a shower for Joshua—he being too old for baths, he stated in no uncertain terms. Both kids were delighted to see Marcello. They immediately wanted to play video games.

"There are no video games," Tree said.

Everyone looked appalled. "What kind of house is this?" Joshua wanted to know.

The boys settled in to watch old YouTube WWE wrestling clips on Tree's computer while Freddie found drawing paper and pencils for Madison, who announced that she aimed to become a dancer and an artist when she grew up.

With the kids settled away, Tree exhausted, slipped into the bedroom and lay down. He had been up all night. He was dead tired. He closed his eyes and the sweet bliss of oncoming sleep began to roll through his body.

Then his cellphone rang.

Tree's eyes popped open. He wouldn't answer it. Couldn't answer it. He answered it.

"Tree, it's Rex," the voice on the line said. "You haven't forgotten about the show tonight, have you?"

22

The crowd was already gathering outside the Big Arts Center when Tree arrived in the tuxedo he had found in a suit bag at the back of his closet and which he had not worn since—well, probably since he attended some long ago awards dinner when he was still at the *Sun-Times*. Much of the crowd, he was surprised to see, was also formally dressed. Sanibel Island residents, it appeared, took their Oscar satires seriously.

He hurried inside and found Rex standing near the stage, elegant in evening wear that fit him like a second skin, relieved when he saw Tree. "Thank goodness," he said. "I was worried you weren't going to show."

"I'm here," Tree said. "But what about Ryde Bodie?"

"What about him?"

"Is he here?"

"He's been here for the last hour," said Rex.

"You're kidding. Where is he?"

"He's backstage," Rex said. "With the other cast members, all of whom showed up on time, as I specifically asked them to. We're just about ready to go, Tree, so please take your seat over there at the end of the row."

"But—"

"This is no time to argue, the show's about to begin," Rex said impatiently. "Sit down."

Tree did as he was told, still in disbelief that Ryde had actually shown up. As the lights in the auditorium dimmed, Tree took a quick look around. To his surprise, the seats in the auditorium were full—an elegant-looking crowd of a certain age, as Tree now thought of his peers. He pulled out the piece of doggerel he had prepared for this evening, and immediately felt better: *Good grief, they told me to be brief...But there are so many people who deserve my thanks...From Steven Spielberg to Tom Hanks...*

Yes, his speech would knock the audience dead, no question. Once again he mused about his failure to pursue an acting career. Why had he not? If he had become a famous actor, beloved by audiences around the world, then he would not have to put up with the body-numbing hardships brought about by his ridiculous decision to become a detective. What had he been thinking, anyway? The smell of the greasepaint. The roar of the crowd. That's what should have drawn him. He'd wasted his life in journalism, a profession that had unceremoniously tossed him onto the street the moment it felt it didn't need him any longer.

The applause as Rex made his entrance onstage pulled him out of his reverie. Rex stepped smartly to the microphone. He seemed right at home.

"I attended those other Academy Awards in Los Angeles for the first time in 1962," he said. "My date was Joan Crawford. That was also the last time I attended the Academy Awards. The next year Joan wasn't talking to me, and somehow my work as Captain Hobart in *G.I. Blues* was overlooked by the Academy. So, tonight I'm finally back and I'm on Sanibel Island, my favorite place in the world—among the people I love most."

Everyone broke into applause. Rex beamed. He was in his element, Tree thought, exactly the place where he should be—in front of an audience, adored.

"And tonight," Rex went on, "we're going to add a few of the things generally missing from the Oscars these days—humor and movie stars. In order to ensure star power at this show, we've called on a few legends from the past—like, for example, Miss Judy Garland!"

More enthusiastic handclapping greeted the arrival of a tiny woman in a sequined evening gown who threw herself into the role of a middle-aged Judy lamenting the fact that she had never won an Academy Award. A wrestling match ensued when Judy presented the best actress Oscar and then tried to hang onto it. Then Rex introduced a tall islander who was, for a few moments, Clark Gable, followed by James Bond, complete with two lovely island women—on walkers. That brought down the house.

Rex returned to the microphone to introduce Fred Astaire and Ginger Rogers who would present the night's award for best actor. Tree tensed, not only because this was his big moment, but also because he could not believe Ryde Bodie, having disappeared so effectively from Lee Memorial Hospital, would—or could—make an appearance.

But a moment later, there he was, a beauty in black tie, gliding with surprising gracefulness onto the stage accompanied by Bonnie, his "Ginger." She looked stunning in a form-fitting silver sheath. Ryde twirled her around the stage in a fair imitation of what the original Fred and Ginger might have accomplished on the dance floor. He did not look like a man who had recently been shot. Anything but, in fact. The dance ended with the two of them in front of the microphone, Ryde flashing that irresistible grin he could haul out for such occasions. Tree was on his feet, heart pounding, headed for his big moment in the spotlight.

He climbed the steps onto the stage. Vaguely, he heard Ryde announce the name of the year's best actor. It didn't matter who it was, as Ryde was pointing out. That guy could not be here tonight, "so accepting the award is Sanibel's preeminent private detective—in fact its *only* private detective, Tree Callister!"

Tree was aware of Ryde stepping away so that now the microphone was directly in front of him, shining through the darkness surrounding the stage. The audience was out there—*his* audience, waiting to be dazzled.

Wait, though.

He looked around. Where was his Oscar statuette? He didn't have his Oscar. Ryde hadn't given him the Oscar. He glanced at Ryde and at Bonnie, so exquisite in that shimmering gown. They looked back at him blankly.

He didn't have the Oscar. That's all he could think. He leaned close to the microphone, opening his mouth to deliver the speech that would bring the audience to its feet with its wit and eloquence.

His mouth was open but nothing was coming out. His mind had gone blank. He could not think of a single word that he had rehearsed. He tried again. His mouth was moving, he was certain of that. But it refused to let any words break free.

The next thing, Ryde was at Tree's side, shoving the Oscar into his sweating hands, and throwing his arm around Tree saying into the microphone, "These darned actors, they can't say anything unless it's written down for them. As an actor, well, Tree's a great detective."

Amid laughter and applause, Ryde led Tree back down the steps and off the stage. Tree was numb. He could not feel anything, and all he could hear was the loud buzzing sound in his head. He seemed to be floating, no longer quite in this place—wishing he was anywhere else in the world.

23

"What happened to you?" Rex demanded after the show. "They didn't give me my Oscar," Tree said lamely.

"What?" Rex said.

"Ryde should have presented me with the Oscar. He didn't do it."

"You promised me you were going to be great."

"When they didn't give me the Oscar, it threw me off," Tree said.

Rex said, "You were the worst thing in the show."

Then Ryde was at Tree's side, grinning that grin, and patting Tree on the back saying, "Hey, buddy, it worked out fine up there."

"You didn't give me the Oscar," Tree said.

Rex said to Ryde, "You were fantastic. That dance with Ginger? Fred himself would have been pleased."

Ryde grinned some more and gave an aw-shucks shrug that made Tree's blood boil. Around him, everyone was congratulating one another. Everyone had delivered on stage. Everyone had remembered their lines. The show had gone off without a hitch. The audience loved it. Everyone was delighted.

Everyone but Tree Callister.

Tree Callister had screwed up. He kept replaying the moment he froze on stage. Damn! He wanted to do it over again. He could recall his speech clearly now. He would really wow the audience this time. Rex just had to give him one more chance, that's all.

"Come on, buddy, it wasn't that bad," Ryde said. Once again he patted Tree's shoulder reassuringly—only it wasn't reassuring at all.

"I've got to talk to you," Tree said.

"I know. I should have given you the Oscar. My bad."

"Not about that, Ryde. About what happened to you."

"What happened to me?" Ryde give him another of the quizzical looks that had become his trademark whenever Tree asked him a question. "I'm not sure what you mean."

"You disappeared from the hospital."

"I didn't disappear. I checked myself out."

He put his hand on Tree's shoulder and seemed to lean against him a moment. He had gone abruptly pale.

"Are you okay?" Tree asked.

"A little pain, that's all."

"Because there is a bullet in you."

He managed a grin. "It only hurts when I breathe." He leaned harder against Tree. "Listen, buddy, do me a favor will you? Part of the reason I wanted to be here tonight, you're right, we do need to talk. Walk me out to my car."

"I should get you back to the hospital," Tree said.

"Let's try for the car, first." The smile was more pained this time.

They moved together through the crowded auditorium, everyone wanting to shake Ryde's hand and tell him what a great job he had done. Amid the shower of compliments, the rosy glow of a man getting lots of attention replaced Ryde's paleness. The praise brought him a new energy. No one said anything to Tree, though. He felt sick to his stomach.

They got outside and went down the ramp into the parking lot. Absent the compliments, Ryde had gone pale again, and he leaned even harder against Tree. "Ryde, you need to get to the hospital," Tree said.

"That's not such a great idea right now," Ryde said. "Right now I need you to come with me and not ask a lot of questions."

"About what?"

"About where we're going."

"Where are we going?"

"There you go asking questions."

Ryde guided Tree over to his Cadillac Escalade. "Do you mind driving, buddy?"

He slipped into the front passenger seat with a grunt of pain while Tree worked his way behind the wheel of the Cadillac. Ryde handed him the key and Tree started the engine.

"I appreciate this buddy, I really do," Ryde said.

"I know you don't want me asking questions like 'where are we going?' But, where are we going?"

"There are some people I want you to meet," Ryde Bodie said.

24

Once the Escalade cleared the causeway, it came along San Carlos Boulevard, Tree careful to keep the vehicle within the speed limit.

"I can't understand it," he said.

"Understand what?" Ryde said.

"I knew my lines. I felt very confident, but then I got up there and I completely froze. My mind went blank. I couldn't think of anything I was supposed to say."

"Tree," Ryde said gently.

"What?"

"Right now we have more pressing problems than your performance at the Big Arts Center."

"Let's talk about something else, then."

"Okay," Ryde said.

"Let's talk about WGE International."

Ryde kept his eyes on the road.

"At first I thought it was Wayne Granger Enterprises," Tree said.

Ryde shook his head. "No, that's not what it stands for."

"Turns out it's a guy named Wally Garrison. But you are also involved with WGE."

"I *was* associated with the company, yes. The founder is dead. The company has been closed down."

"It was selling motor vehicle retail installment contracts."

"The company offered a variety of financial products."

"Jim Waterhouse seemed to think the company had defrauded him."

"Waterhouse was a blowhard fool," Ryde said.

"Who is now dead."

Ryde threw a glance at Tree. "What? You think I killed Jim Waterhouse?"

"Did you?"

"It looks to me like Waterhouse set my house on fire because he was trying to get back at me and died in the blaze. End of story."

"What about the federal government?"

"The federal government? What's the government got to do with anything?"

"The feds are investigating you, aren't they?"

Ryde said, "I don't know, Tree. Are they?"

"Does the investigation have to do with your involvement in WGE?"

"I have no idea," Ryde said.

There was no more to say—well, there was, but neither of them chose to say anything further as they came over the bridge and along Estero Boulevard. Clusters of young people floated between the bars and the restaurants. The porch at Hooters was jammed and noisy, everyone in Fort Myers Beach having a great time—everyone except Tree Callister.

Tree Callister was feeling very sorry for himself tonight.

It wasn't long before the lights and the crowds began to fade, and the quiet of the Florida night asserted itself. The aging residents slept soundly in the condo towers crowding either side of the boulevard, oblivious to the fact that one of their brethren, the aging Big Arts Center screw-up, Tree Callister, was adrift in the night, once again headed into deep, troubled water.

That water appeared to be located at the place Tree suspected it might be—the marina behind the Santini Plaza. The Cadillac's headlights lit the iron skeleton on the boat storage units as it bumped onto the roadway above the docks. *El Trueno*, shimmering in the night, was back in its berth.

Tree exited the Escalade. Ryde was already outside. "Here we are," Ryde said. He was holding his side again. In the dim light, he looked paler than ever.

"What is this?"

"Just be patient, Tree."

Tree followed Ryde across the roadway onto the dock. Approaching the yacht, someone stirred on the rear deck and Manuel, the short man who had accompanied Paola at Ryde's Rabbit Road house, came into view.

He said, "Qué pasa, Ryde?"

To which Ryde replied, "Me duele el corazón, Manuel."

The short man named Manuel just stared at him.

Diego materialized out of the darkness beside Manuel. He snarled something in Spanish. He did not appear to be happy to see either of them.

They boarded the yacht and then followed Manuel into a spacious, softly-lit cabin. As soon as they got inside, Paola came through an adjacent door. Paola's forehead was bandaged. The side of her face was a purplish smear from Tommy's fist. She was dressed in black jeans and a black formless pullover. Her hatchet face showed no emotion but she rubbed gently at her bruise as she inspected these new arrivals in their formal gear. In guttural Spanish, she addressed Ryde.

He turned to Tree. "What did you do to her?"

"I hit her."

"You hit Paola? With your fist?"

"No. With a gun."

"A gun? I thought you didn't have a gun."

"I don't. It was her gun."

"I see," Ryde said.

"Before that, someone else hit her with his fist," Tree said.

"You should not have done that," Ryde said.

Paola, still nursing the side of her face, once again spoke in Spanish. In any language, she sounded as unhappy as Diego—and she kept glaring at Tree.

Manuel addressed Ryde in English: "This is the man you spoke of? This is the man who will help you?"

For a moment, Tree wasn't sure who Manuel was talking about.

"That's correct," Ryde said.

"Me?" Tree blurted. "How am I supposed to help you?"

Ryde said, "I'm sorry I got you involved in this, buddy."

Tree was about to say something like "involved in what?" when Paola stepped forward, gesticulating dramatically and speaking rapidly in Spanish. "What's she saying?" Tree demanded.

"She wants to know what you did with the children," Ryde said, an unaccustomed edge of uncertainty in his voice. "You have Joshua and Madison?"

"I know where they are," Tree said. "They're safe."

Ryde looked at him, and for the first time there was something like amazement on his face. "But *you* have Madison and Joshua?"

"What? You would rather she has them?"

"That was part of the deal, yeah."

"You're kidding," Tree said.

"No, Tree, I'm not."

"What kind of deal was that?"

Instead of answering, Ryde turned to Paola and once again addressed her in a burst of Spanish. When he finished, she moved closer to Tree, baring her teeth in the same savage snarl she had produced back in Everglades City. Not a pleasant sight. It sent a cold chill down his spine. This hatchet-faced little woman was genuinely scary. She spoke to him in English, the words coming out in a breathless hiss: "I don't like you."

That brought Manuel into play. "You should not have hit her," he said to Tree, also in English.

"She had a gun," Tree said.

"You should not have hit her with her gun."

"I wasn't thinking," Tree said.

"But you will make amends," he said, "by giving us the money."

"What money?" Tree said. Every word out of his mouth since he met Ryde Bodie seemed to have a question mark attached to it.

Paola, studying Tree the way she might study a dead animal at the side of the road, sputtered away in Spanish, spitting out the words between her clenched teeth.

Manuel helpfully translated: "She says the money you will pay us for the life of your friend and his children. The money you keep hidden and will not miss because you cannot spend it, anyway."

Tree looked at Ryde in horror. "What the hell money is *that*?"

Manuel answered: "The nine million dollars."

The look of horror turned to astonishment. Tree opened his mouth to announce loudly that he did not have nine million dollars, but something inside him, a warning voice, cautioned against such a vehement protest, a protest that could only place him in more danger—if he did not have nine million dollars, what was the point of him?

So he said nothing.

Manuel actually managed a smile, his eyes filling with admiration. "You are one of us, as it turns out. A man who appears to be the one thing, but who is actually the other, secret thing. That kind of man, he takes what he wants. So you will give us the money, because we know you now, and what you give us, you will surely take from someone else, so no one loses."

Yes, they certainly know me, Tree thought. Good old crooked Tree. He never guessed he was so transparent.

Paola held up four fingers and muttered words in Spanish.

"She give you four days," Manuel said. "You return in four days. Bring the money in cash, and the debt is paid."

Ryde's smile was uneasy, its wattage greatly reduced. "Really appreciate this, buddy."

Paola's eyes flashed again and thin lips yawned open, spitting out more angry Spanish. Tree looked at Manuel, who shrugged helplessly. "Yes, yes. Paola says that if you do not have the money by then, not only will we kill this man beside you and his children, we will also kill you and your wife."

25

Dimly, Tree was aware of Diego steering them back along the dock to the roadway and the waiting Escalade. All he could think of was Paola's animal-like snarl, and Manuel's offhand threat to kill not only him but Freddie, too. This could not be possible, he thought. He could not have once again put Freddie's life in danger. He could not possibly get into messes like this over and over again.

Except he could.

When they arrived at the Escalade, Diego swung around to Ryde, pushing his face very close. "They may be willing to let you off, but I am not," he declared through clenched teeth. Ryde appeared to have a knack for encouraging everyone to speak to him with their teeth clenched.

"You find your own way back," he grunted before marching away to the Escalade.

He climbed inside, started the engine, and a moment later drove off. Ryde shook his head. "Can you believe that guy?" He had his cellphone out, tapping at the keys on its glass surface. He looked up at Tree. "You all right there, buddy?"

"Ryde, I'm not your buddy, and I'm not all right. What's wrong with Diego? Why is he so pissed off?"

"He's got the wrong idea about Rodrigo."

"Rodrigo? Who's Rodrigo?"

"Rodrigo Ramos. Diego's twin brother. A much nicer guy than Diego, I have to say. They're Paola's cousins." Ryde concentrated on his cellphone.

"This is the guy who washed up on Captiva Island?"

"That's him."

"You killed him?"

"Diego *thinks* I killed him."

"What did you tell them about me?"

Ryde was still poking at his cellphone. "Look, I'm sorry, but that whole deal at the house changed the equation. Paola thinks that hit man was hired by one of her rivals to kill all of us at the dinner party, so suddenly I'm radioactive."

"What's any of this got to do with me?"

"I told them you stole nine million dollars."

"Are you crazy? Why did you tell them that?"

Ryde stopped working his cellphone. "Because that's what you did."

Tree stared at Ryde in shocked disbelief. "What makes you think so?"

"Come on, buddy. You're sitting on the nine million."

"How would you know?"

"Let's move," Ryde said. He started away, walking toward the shopping center, holding his side once again.

Tree hurried after him. "You didn't answer me," he called. "Who told you I had nine million?"

They crossed the Santini Marina Plaza parking lot and Ryde came to a stop at the edge of Estero Boulevard. Across the street, a 7-Eleven shone through the night, the only sign of life. Ryde took a deep breath and grimaced.

"You need to get some help," Tree said.

"You keep saying that, buddy, and I'm gonna start to believe you."

"And who exactly are these people—Diego and Manuel, and my favorite, Paola?"

Ryde shrugged. "Business associates. They think I owe them money."

"They *think* you owe them money?"

"I don't, of course. It's this WGE thing we talked about earlier. They don't seem to understand that some investments pay off and others don't. But with these people, better to pay them than argue. Paola will take the nine million and call it even."

"And supposing I didn't steal nine million, Ryde? Supposing what you heard about me isn't true? Then what?"

"Then we're in trouble, buddy." Ryde was looking at his watch. "But you've got the money," he added confidently. "I'm counting on you."

Abruptly, they were bathed in the light of an approaching car. Tree thought it would pass, but instead the car, a red Lexus, slowed and pulled into the 7-Eleven.

"Look, I've gotta split," Ryde said.

"You've got to what?" Once again Tree found himself shaking his head in disbelief.

"You've got your cellphone, right? Freddie will pick you up."

Tree looked across the way at the Lexus. Bonnie was behind the wheel. She waved at them and suddenly Tree realized who she was.

"Bonnie is Wally Garrison's wife, isn't she?"

"Bonnie and Wally were married, yeah," Ryde acknowledged. "But Wally's gone now, and Bonnie's all alone. I'll see you later, Tree."

"You're not going anywhere."

"Come on, buddy, don't be like that. You said it yourself. I've gotta get some help."

"You're not walking away from this."

"I'm not walking away, I'm being driven. I don't want to keep Bonnie waiting. I'll be in touch."

Tree moved to block him. "You're not leaving," he said.

Ryde looked exasperated. "Don't play the tough guy, Tree. The part doesn't fit. I don't want to go into a lot of detail, but I'm a former Green Beret, and they trained me to kill people and a lot of other ugly stuff that I really don't want to bore you with. The point being, you can't stop me, and you're only going to get yourself hurt if you try."

"You know, Ryde," Tree replied, "I'm getting tired of all your lies and evasions. You stay right here with me until we figure out what to do about all this."

Tree wasn't sure in retrospect what Ryde did, but the next thing he found himself down on the pavement, gasping for breath. Ryde stood over him, saying, "Sorry, buddy. I really didn't want to do that."

Then he loped across the road and got into the Lexus. Bonnie gunned the vehicle back along Estero.

Tree got uncertainly to his feet, holding his stomach, fighting to maintain his balance against a sea breeze rising, the silence of the night descending.

26

Wonderful Freddie without (too much) complaint came to pick him up, mystified that a husband who had started off in a tuxedo for a show at the Big Arts Center had ended up in Fort Myers Beach.

"Thank you," he said after she found him sitting forlornly at the roadside, holding his stomach.

"It's not every night I get to pick up a guy in a tux on the side of the road. Incidentally, why are you holding your stomach?"

"Someone hit it with a fist."

"Why would someone do that?"

Tree said, "It's a long story."

Crossing San Carlos Bridge he told her what had happened. He told her everything—or at least everything he knew, which, when it came right down to it, was not a whole lot.

"But you don't have nine million dollars," she said.

He hesitated perhaps a second or two longer than he should have before he answered, "No."

She cast him a sidelong glance—there were sidelong glances each time the subject of nine million dollars came up. "Tree, why is there always this hesitancy before you answer that question?"

"There is no hesitancy," he said.

"There is," she maintained.

"You are imagining things."

"I wish I was, but I don't think I am."

"The point is," Tree said, "it doesn't matter really whether I have it or I don't, too many people think I do, including people who say they are willing to kill us if I don't come up with it."

"What are you going to do?"

"I've got four days to figure that out," Tree said.

"Who are these people, anyway?"

"Whoever they are, they are not nice."

"And who is Ryde Bodie or Wayne Granger or whatever his name is, and how has he ended up in this predicament? For that matter, how did you end up in it?"

"We can blame Marcello for that," Tree said.

"Or you can take some personal responsibility here, and decide you are going to walk away from these things and not walk into them."

"Yes, I can decide to do that, I suppose," Tree agreed. "Except right now I'm in it, and I've got no choice but to figure the way out."

"Let me ask you this," Freddie said. "If you did have the money, would you give it to them?"

"That's supposing I have it."

"Let's suppose."

"I'm not so sure giving them the money would save us or Ryde Bodie," Tree said.

"I'm scared, Tree," Freddie said.

"Yes," Tree said, "I am, too. And I haven't even told you the worst part of it."

"What's that?"

"I totally sucked doing the Oscar show tonight."

"Tree—"

"It's no use trying to reassure me," he said. "I got up on the stage, and I looked out at the audience, and I totally froze. Couldn't remember a thing."

"Tree, it's—"

"Please, don't tell me it's all right."

"I wasn't going to tell you that," Freddie said.

"What were you going to tell me?"

"I was going to tell you that, right now, you've got bigger problems."

───────────

When they arrived back at Andy Rosse Lane, Tommy, holding an ice pack against his swollen hand, was on the sofa watching WWE clips on the iPad, Madison and Joshua huddled on either side of him with Marcello trying hard to look as though he was far too mature for snuggling.

"Josh and I both love Rey Mysterio," Tommy said.

"I don't like wrestling," Madison declared.

Marcello, not looking at all happy, got off the sofa and came over to Tree. "I thought we were partners."

"We're temporary partners," Tree amended.

"So, temporary partner, what happened tonight?"

Tommy had lost interest in the iPad. "Something happened tonight?"

"I think something did," Marcello said.

"It's late," Freddie announced. "You kids should be in bed by now."

"They just wanted to watch one more match," Tommy said.

"And one more and one more," Madison said in a bored voice.

Marcello addressed Tree. "So you're not going to tell me?"

"There's nothing to tell," Tree said. "I went to the Oscar show. Here I am home again."

"Where's your car?" Marcello demanded. "How come Freddie had to go and pick you up?"

Tommy gave Tree a closer look. "You look as though you've been put through the wringer, Mr. C. What happened tonight? Are you okay?"

"I don't think I'm cut out for a life in show business," Tree said.

"We can talk about this later," Freddie said. "Right now everyone has to get some sleep." Adopting the no-nonsense tone employed when she was not in the mood to argue.

Tommy said he would get the kids into bed. A chorus of objections briefly arose from Madison and Joshua, but once again Freddie put that authoritative voice to work and the three kids trooped off, accompanied by Tommy who promised to tuck them in—Marcello protesting that he was too old to be tucked in.

Tree could not remember the last time he slept. His whole body ached with exhaustion. He undressed. Freddie asked him if he wanted anything to eat. He shook his head and sank onto the edge of bed. All he wanted right now was sleep.

He rolled under the covers. Freddie loomed over him, the uncertain light framing the loving expression on her face. "What am I going to do with you?" she said to him. "You're going to get yourself killed."

"They can't kill me," he said. "I'm the hero of the story."

"Heroes get killed all the time," Freddie said. "And let's face it you're not *that* much of a hero."

"No, I suppose not."

That was the last thing he remembered saying.

———

A brightly-lit cinderblock corridor reverberated with the distant roar of a crowd. Tree went along the corridor, through a series of connecting doors, until he encountered a man in a red windbreaker. The man wore sunglasses. Tree marveled at his artfully arranged blown-dry hair.

The man in the red jacket said, "The mayor's just been here and presented him with some sort of plaque. And a native kid. There's a native kid. At least I think she's native."

"Native?" said Tree.

"Yeah. She gave him something, too. He's sweating a lot tonight. Waiting for you."

"For me?" Tree said.

The man with the blown-dry hair shrugged and the overhead light glinted off his sunglasses as he opened the door behind him. Tree stepped into a team dressing room with exposed overhead pipes and benches in front of walls lined with metal lockers. A fat man sat on one of the benches. He had jet black hair pushed up in a pompadour. Jet black sideburns framed a pale, fleshy face all but lost in the high collar that was part of the white, spangled jump suit he wore—a jump suit that strained to contain his heavy torso. The fat man's small, heavily-lidded eyes were outlined in what looked like eyeliner. He squinted, and his fingers twitched spasmodically.

"Grab one of those tissues over there," he said to Tree, pointing to a box of Kleenex on a nearby bench.

Tree went over and pulled out two or three tissues and returned to the fat man in the white jump suit.

"Just dab my face, will you? I'm sweating like crazy."

Tree used the tissue to catch the perspiration running down his cheeks.

"Are you all right?" Tree said.

"Yeah, I'm fine. Tired, that's all. Tired a lot, lately. I'm not sleeping, always trouble sleeping. I've gotta go out there in a few minutes and do a concert, although I'm not even sure where we are. Rapid City?"

"We've met before," Tree said.

"I meet a lot of people, sir."

"You drove a golf cart on a sound stage. It was late. You were having trouble sleeping then, too."

"I've always had trouble. That's why I take medication. So I can sleep. That and the colds. I seem to get colds a lot." He became silent. Tree pressed a tissue against his damp forehead.

"Yeah, I think we're in Rapid City," the fat man said. "What is it, early June? And you say we've met before?"

"That's right," Tree said.

"Well, I got a couple of months left, but, sir, you're not going to make it that long."

Tree stopped dabbing at the white, sweaty face. "What do you mean?"

"Don't stop, okay? I can't go out there sweating like a pig."

Tree used the tissue to pat the fat man's high forehead, gathering the moisture running along his scalp line. The fat man said, "That's what I wanted to tell you. They're gonna kill you. That's all they wrote for you, son."

"This is crazy," Tree said. "How would you know when I'm going to die?"

"It's this whole spiritualism thing I'm into. I can see things others can't. What's the word when you can do that? When you can see the future, that sort of thing?"

"Prescient?"

"That's it. Something like that. I know what you're thinking. You're thinking you can somehow dodge the trouble you're in. Well, forget that. Sir, these people you're dealing with, they're snakes. They kill meaner people than you before breakfast. They don't care."

"I don't believe it," Tree said.

"Believe it or not, that's up to you. The fact is neither one of us is gonna make it, so there you go. Wherever we're going, Heaven, the Great Beyond, whatever, it's got to be better than this."

"This is all right," Tree said. "I don't mind this so much. It has its drawbacks, sure. But I have a beautiful, loving wife, good friends, a home on an island a lot of people think is paradise. I've really got a lot to live for when I think about it."

"Then why do you keep figuring out new ways to get yourself killed? What makes you want to throw it all away?"

"Do you think that's what I'm doing? Throwing it all away?"

"Don't you?"

"I don't know," Tree said, perplexed. "I guess I'd never thought of it quite that way."

"I hope those gospel hymns I sang all my life are true. I just want to see my mama again, that's all." He gave an ironic smile. "Ever since she died, it hasn't been the same. We should be living in paradise but paradise turns out to be hell on earth."

"It's not hell," Tree protested. "I don't think it's hell—most of the time, I don't think that."

"I told myself the same thing for a long time. But the darkness keeps coming in, and now it's the end. You're old and I'm fat, and we're both going down."

"What happened to you, anyway?"

"What happened to both of us, sir? How did we end up sitting in a dressing room that smells like dirty socks in Rapid City, South Dakota? We were both something else, and now we're this, in a place we never intended to be, filled with regrets. We both could've done it differently, I guess, but the fact is we didn't, so here we are."

From outside, Tree could hear music start up, the strains of Strauss's *Also sprach Zarathustra*. The entrance door opened, and more men in red jackets with blown-dry hair filed in. "It's time, Boss," one of the men said.

"Gotta go." The fat man in the white suit rose to his feet. One of the red-jacketed men took over Tree's job wiping the sweat on the fat man's forehead.

Tree stood up. "I wish I knew what to say to you."

"Hey, just give me a hug."

Tree embraced him. The fat man's whole body felt damp.

In the background, the music was rising toward a crescendo. Tree and the fat man in the white suit shook hands. "Hope you make it, sir."

"You, too," Tree said.

"I don't think it looks good for either of us," he said. "But I suppose we can dream, can't we?"

"Yes," Tree said. "We can always dream."

"Dream what?" Freddie said.

Tree opened his eyes. Freddie said, "It's morning. You slept in."

27

"You sure sleep a lot," Madison observed when Tree finally padded out of the bedroom, into the kitchen. She was seated at the table in a pink bathing suit, holding a red pencil poised over drawing paper, her hair still wet from an early morning visit to the beach.

"Since I met you and your brother, I haven't had any sleep at all," Tree said.

Madison concentrated on drawing her picture. "Thomas took us to the beach," she announced as she worked away. "He's nice."

Because Tree had not taken them to the beach, he was not nice. He could not disagree. "Where did you get the bathing suit?" he inquired.

"Freddie got it for me—and one for Joshua, too."

"It looks pretty on you," Tree said, pouring himself a cup of coffee.

"Pink is my favorite color," Madison said, before adding, "Freddie is nice, too."

Tree noted he was the only adult inside the Andy Rosse Lane house this morning not designated by Madison as "nice."

He added milk and then leaned against the counter sipping his coffee. Freddie came in, looking spectacular in her one-piece orange bathing suit, trailed by Tommy, less spectacular in oversized trunks, followed by Joshua and Marcello.

Tommy said, "This taking care of kids is kind of fun."

"Thomas can't swim very well," Joshua confided. "I helped him."

"I swim all right," Tommy protested. "I just need a little encouragement, that's all. Besides, I've got a sore hand." He held up his still-swollen hand as proof.

Freddie said, "The kids want to go back to the beach. Why don't you come along with us, Tree?"

"I don't know that I'm up to ocean swims first thing in the morning," Tree said.

"Come on, Mr. C," Tommy said. "It'll be good for you."

"We should be working this case," Marcello said to Tree.

"How should we be doing this?"

"We should be putting stuff on the walls."

"What kind of stuff?" Tree asked.

"You know, newspaper stories and photographs—maybe those mug shots, too. Drawing arrows that look confusing but help us solve the case."

"Like in the movies," Tree said.

"Yeah, they always do that in the movies," Marcello said.

"Except I don't have any photographs," Tree said.

"And you're not drawing lines on my walls," Freddie said.

"I want to draw the lines," Madison cried. "I want to draw the lines!"

Marcello shook his head in disgust. "No wonder we can't solve this case."

Freddie persisted with the return to the beach, finally leading everyone out except Tree. He finished his coffee and called Rex.

"Even Paul Newman made bad movies," Tree said.

"Paul Newman didn't end up on stage, staring bug-eyed at the audience, his mouth opening, but nothing coming out," Rex said.

"You are very cruel, Rex."

"You may have to give up this idea of becoming an actor."

"You were great last night, incidentally," Tree said. "I should be big enough, in the face of my personal failure, to tell you that."

"You must want something," Rex said. "What is it?"

"Can't I even give you a compliment?"

"You can, but it's because you want something. What is it?"

"Bonnie. Ryde Bodie's dance partner. She's Bonnie Garrison, isn't she?"

"The Widow Garrison," Rex said. "Her husband died last year in Charlotte, just as the FBI was about to indict him."

"Wonderful Wally," Tree said. "Bonnie lives here on the island, right?"

"Bonnie has a place on West Gulf Drive. She's fighting the feds to hang onto it."

"Why would the feds want it?"

"Because the government believes the house is part of the proceeds from the Ponzi scheme her husband cooked up."

"So you know about Wonderful Wally and his car contracts."

"I don't know the details. Bonnie says they have been investigating her, but she claims she had no idea what Wally was up to. She just thought he was a brilliant businessman."

"You talked to her about this?"

"Unlike some other people I know, Bonnie actually showed up for the rehearsals when she was supposed to. We got to talking." There was a pause and then Rex said, "I think there's something going on between Ryde Bodie and Bonnie."

"You don't happen to have Bonnie's address on West Gulf Drive, do you?"

"See?" Rex said with a sigh. "I knew you wanted something."

The canary yellow frame house stood at the end of a long paved road off West Gulf Drive. The house was built atop stilts, the steps and porch area painted a chocolate brown so that a first-time visitor would have no difficulty locating the front door.

Tree had taken a taxi to retrieve the Beetle from the Big Arts Center parking lot. Now he parked and climbed the steps and rang the doorbell. No one answered. He rang it again. Still no answer. He tried the door. It was locked. He went down the steps and around to the back to a second brown-painted porch. Two big windows overlooked the ocean, but nobody in the house wanted to see the ocean today. Blinds were drawn across the windows. He knocked on the back door. Still, no one answered. This time, however, when he tried the door, it opened.

Tree leaned in and called out. "Hello? Anyone home?"

The silence of the house came back at him. He could hear insect sounds from outside, but otherwise there was nothing. His stomach began to twist into a knot. He called again: "Bonnie? It's Tree Callister. Are you here?"

Getting no reply, he stepped into a kitchen area, his stomach tightening even more. He should just turn around and walk out and forget he was ever here. Instead, he moved through the white kitchen with its white cupboards and white marble countertops. The living room-dining room area was white, too, beneath a slant roof. A white fan overhung furniture that was like an afterthought, added by people on vacation with better things to do. The enormous black eye of a flat screen television followed his every move.

Bonnie Garrison lay curled beneath a flowered duvet on a king-size bed in the master bedroom. At first he thought she was asleep—he prayed she was asleep.

"Bonnie," he said. "It's me, Bonnie. Tree Callister."

She did not respond. He steeled himself and stepped over to the bed and yanked back the covers. Bonnie lay on her side, naked and unmoving. He touched her skin. It was cold and hard. Rigor mortis had set in.

There was no blood and no sign of how Bonnie Garrison might have died. Just a dead woman lying on her side in a bedroom on a sunny morning.

Tree stood staring down at her, numb, resisting again the urge to flee. He had done this too many times, found too many dead bodies.

Then he noticed the single flower lying on the bedside table—a black iris.

His cellphone rang. He fished it from his pocket. A voice said, "Tree? It's me. Ryde."

"Where are you?"

"I'm in trouble."

"Yes. I'm at Bonnie Garrison's house."

There was a long silence before Ryde said, "What are you doing there?"

"What do you think I'm doing? I'm looking for you."

"Don't go inside," he said.

"Too late, I'm already inside."

"Oh, God." As desperate as Tree had ever heard Ryde Bodie sound. "Listen to me, Tree. Okay? I didn't kill her. I want you to know that."

"Where are you now?" Tree asked.

"I came back from a run on the beach and I went into the bedroom, Tree, and she was like that. I swear she was."

"Then what makes you so sure someone killed her?"

"What are you talking about? She's dead. Someone must have killed her."

"There's a black iris lying on a side table," Tree said. "I've seen it before. Do you have any idea what it means?"

"Yes," he said, his voice rising excitedly. "It was Paola and her bunch. That's their calling card. It must have been them. They must have come to the house looking for me."

"You need to get back here, Ryde. We can phone the police and tell them what happened."

"That's the thing, Tree. I've already called the police."

"When did you do that?"

"Minutes ago. A few minutes ago. They should be there any time now."

Tree looked out the bedroom window just as the first of three police cruisers turned off West Gulf Drive, headed toward the house.

"Ryde," Tree said into the receiver.

But Ryde was gone, and the police were pounding at the back door.

28

Tree emerged from the bedroom just as two officers with shaved heads burst into the kitchen, Glock pistols held in the department-sanctioned combat grip. Tree recognized one of the cops: T.J. Hanks was the officer who had stopped him on the way to rehearsal at the Big Arts Center.

In unison, the officers screamed at him to keep his hands where they could see them and to get down on the floor. Tree tried to tell them he was a private detective working a case, but they weren't interested. They just kept yelling, fingers on the triggers of the Glock, thumbs straight, ready to do the serious business of pumping him full of lead. He got to his knees, and T.J. Hanks moved forward. He pushed Tree down on his face before yanking his arms behind him and snapping handcuffs on his wrists.

Meanwhile, the second officer, adopting a shooter's crouch, ducked into the bedroom. Tree could hear him call out, "Ma'am? Ma'am? Are you all right, ma'am?" That was followed by an explosion of swear words—the officer discovering that Bonnie Garrison was dead. The second officer reappeared from the bedroom, paler and more bug-eyed than before, shouting something into the radio microphone clipped to his chest.

Then T.J. Hanks was yelling in Tree's ear, "What did you do to her? What did you do?" And Tree was trying to say he didn't do anything. By now additional uniformed officers had entered the house, everyone milling around in confusion.

Hanks and the second officer lifted Tree to his feet and hustled him outside and down the backstairs to their cruiser. The officers unceremoniously shoved Tree into the backseat and then left him there, hands cuffed behind him.

Tree sat uncomfortably, watching as the usual array of emergency vehicles streamed up the road to the yellow house. Even a fire truck showed up. Everyone wanted to be part of a possible homicide on Sanibel Island.

T. J. Hanks reappeared and climbed into the front seat holding a clipboard. Calmer now, Hanks asked Tree to explain what he was doing at the house. If he recognized Tree from their previous encounter, he gave no sign. Tree said he was on a case and Bonnie's name had come up in connection with it. He knew her from the Big Arts Center and decided to drop around and ask her a few questions. When he arrived, there was no answer at the front door. He went around to the back, found the rear door open, became worried when there was still no answer, and entered and found Bonnie in the bedroom.

Hanks made careful notes on the clipboard with a ballpoint pen. When Tree was finished, the officer grunted something Tree didn't understand and left the car. Tree sat there for ten more minutes before he saw a familiar brown Buick come up the drive to join the growing armada parked around the house. Cee Jay Boone and Owen Markfield got out and were met by T.J. Hanks. Tree watched as the three huddled together. Hanks gestured toward the car with Tree inside.

Abruptly, Markfield, his face reddening and twisting into an expression of anger Tree knew well, broke away and charged at the cruiser. He yanked open the rear door, shouting, "What the hell do you think you're doing?" He grabbed at Tree's shirt and jerked him forward before dragging him from the car.

Tree landed on the ground with such force it knocked the wind out of him. Vaguely, he could hear Markfield yelling, although he could no longer make out the words. Markfield grabbed him by the arms and hauled him away from the cruiser across a grassy patch into a tangle of bushes. Then Markfield began kicking him. Tree, his hands bound behind him, frantically tried to roll away, but Markfield made sure Tree didn't get far.

Eventually—only a couple of minutes had elapsed, but it seemed forever—through a veil of pain, Tree became aware of Cee Jay yelling to "stop this." Trying to hold Markfield back. She was soon aided by T.J. Hanks. Surprising—Tree thought for sure Hanks would prefer to join in the kicking.

It was Hanks who finally managed to pull the enraged Markfield away. Cee Jay knelt down to Tree, and said, "Hey. Are you all right?"

No. Not really, Tree thought. But he decided that a non-committal grunt was best at this point.

He noticed officers watching blank faced from a distance, as if hesitant to get too close to the object of Markfield's rage, although from the look of some of the cops, they would not have minded giving him a kick or two themselves.

Cee Jay shifted him around, did something to his bound hands and the next thing the handcuffs came off and he was being lifted into a sitting position.

"We better get him to hospital," Tree heard Cee Jay say. This from the woman who once tried to kill him. Their relationship was evolving, he decided.

"He's all right," someone said. That was more like it, Tree thought through the enveloping pain.

He no sooner thought this, than somehow he was on the ground again surrounded by a trio of emergency medical workers, two young males and a slim, freckled female. They took turns snapping questions, beginning with, "Tree? Can you hear me, Tree?"

Loud and clear he thought, although when he opened his mouth to say this, he wasn't certain anything came out.

That was a moment before everything, curiously, turned pink—why would the world become pink, he wondered—and Tree ceased to worry about saying anything.

29

When Tree regained consciousness, and tried to lift his arms, he discovered his wrists were bound in restraints attached to a hospital bed. A young doctor with blond hair, carefully parted at the side, and with a distracted, professional manner, said, "You don't have a concussion."

"How do you know?" Tree asked.

"I'm a doctor," the doctor said. Of course, Tree thought. That would explain everything.

"Why am I tied to the bed like this?" Tree said.

"Because you are a dangerous criminal," the doctor said. As if being a dangerous criminal was the most natural thing in the world.

"I'm not dangerous," Tree said.

"Says you," replied the doctor.

"Can you tell me what's wrong with me?"

"Yeah, they didn't beat enough of the crap out of you."

The doctor swirled from the room, a bundle of youthful, purposeful energy. Everyone was young, Tree thought. The police were young, the emergency medical people. Everyone but Tree Callister. What did any of them care if a sixtyish private detective survived or not? They had their whole lives ahead of them. Tree was nearing his end, and aching. Let him die at the side of the road, food for the buzzards. Were there buzzards in South Florida?

Cee Jay Boone came into a watery focus. She was a little older than the rest. Maybe she wouldn't feed him to the buzzards.

"Tree," she said. "You are under arrest."

Or maybe not.

"What am I under arrest for?" His voice sounded tired and strained and old.

"Assaulting a police officer and resisting arrest," Cee Jay said. To her credit, she managed to say it with a straight face.

"You know that's not true," Tree said.

"Tree," she continued in a formal voice. "I know you've heard this before, but you do have the right to remain silent. You also have the right to a lawyer, and further, anything you do or say can be held against you in a court of law. Do you understand what I'm telling you?"

"I understand," Tree said.

"And are you willing to answer questions now without an attorney present?"

"No," he said.

"Also," Cee Jay added, "we are holding you as a possible accessory to the murder of Bonnie Garrison."

Tree groaned and said, "Come on, Cee Jay. Why would I kill Bonnie Garrison?"

"The medical examiner thinks she was strangled, but maybe you can help us with that, Tree."

"No, I can't, Cee Jay."

"Suit yourself," she said. "Here's the game plan. They're going to keep you here at Lee Memorial tonight for observation. Then tomorrow we will move you to the Lee County Jail. You'll be held there overnight before being arraigned on the charges I've just outlined to you."

"This is crazy, Cee Jay."

"Is it?" she said. "If that's the case, Tree, start co-operating, and things will get a whole lot less crazy real quick."

"Can I at least see my wife?"

"I want to help you out, Tree, I really do. We've had our differences in the past, I know. But I've actually grown to like you. Even so, I need you to help me before I can do anything for you."

"I told the officers everything I know," Tree said.

"That's not good enough."

"It's all I've got."

Cee Jay offered him a knowing smirk before she departed, leaving him alone with his pain, and giving him plenty of time to mull over the gloomy state of his life. Except his mind was a fuzzy blank. The pain killers did that to him, he suspected. They did everything except kill the pain.

A nurse swished into the room. She looked familiar. "Lindsay?" he said.

She blessed him with a smile. "You've got a pretty good memory there, Mr. Callister."

"How could I forget?"

"You were a visitor the last time I saw you, now you're a patient. How did that happen?"

"I'm lying here trying to figure it out," Tree said.

"The last time you came here you were in charge of security, although I thought you were a little old for that job," Lindsay said. "This time you're a dangerous criminal."

"I'm evolving," Tree said.

"I still think you're a little old," Lindsay said.

"I'm not a little old," Tree said. "I'm too old."

"You're not going to hurt anyone, are you Mr. Callister?"

"I'm too weak and I hurt too much to be much of a threat to anyone."

"That's a relief," she said. "Can I get you anything?"

"How about some water?"

She poured water from a blue pitcher into a plastic glass, and then added a straw which she pressed gently between his parched lips.

"How's that?" she said when he'd had enough to drink.

"Thanks, I appreciate it."

"All part of the service here at Lee County Memorial," Nurse Lindsay said. "I'll come back a little later with your meds. Try to get some rest."

She left the room and Tree closed his eyes. A moment later, he was in a deep sleep.

———————

By the next morning, the pain killers Nurse Lindsay had given Tree began to wear off, and it seemed like every single part of him was on fire. Nonetheless, he was deemed well enough to be transferred over to the Lee County Jail on Dr. Martin Luther King Jr. Boulevard. Nurse Lindsay helped him dress. "Are they really going to put you in jail?" she asked.

"I'm afraid so," he said.

"I've never met a jail bird before," she said.

"You're young," Tree said. "You've got your whole life ahead of you—plenty of opportunity to meet more jail birds."

When she finished getting him dressed, Lindsay said, "Good luck, Mr. Callister."

"Thanks, Lindsay. My experience with jails is that I'm going to need all the luck I can get."

Shortly after that, Tree was shackled and transferred by prison van to the county jail. Once inside, he was told to strip, his street clothes were taken away, and he was outfitted with a red jump suit. Then he was taken to a holding cell filled with inmates similarly clad in red jumpsuits. The cell smelled of a combination of urine and sweat. It was so crowded Tree couldn't find a place to sit down. He finally got a guard's attention, and was allowed out to make a phone call. "You call collect," the guard said. "Four bucks for fifteen minutes."

He telephoned Freddie at work. Did he detect a moment's hesitation before she agreed to accept a collect call from him?

"Where are you?" Freddie said. "I've been frantic."

"Now don't get mad at me," Tree said. "But I'm in the Lee County Jail."

Dead silence and then, "What did you do this time?"

"I didn't do anything—except find Bonnie Garrison's body. What they *say* I did was assault a police officer and resist arrest."

"You can't be serious," Freddie said.

"Listen, I don't have a lot of time to talk, Freddie. Can you call Edith Goldman and tell her what's happened? I'll be arraigned tomorrow morning at which time they will probably set bail. I'll need Edith there, and you, too."

"To write a check, I suppose."

"Unless you want me to rot in jail," Tree said.

"Don't tempt me," Freddie said.

———

"Those were good days," said a man with one lens of his glasses blacked out as Tree was returned to the holding cell. "We were more like businessmen than criminals. We would bring the weed in by boat through the dense mangroves, and the local dealers would take delivery. It seemed as though everyone was involved, so there was very little interference from the authorities."

One of the inmates hanging on the man's words said, "What happened?"

"The Reagan administration happened. That Hollywood actor who could not remember anything unless it was written down for him, he destroyed the business. There were raids and arrests and it just got so much more complicated that we gave it up, and of course everything has become a lot more difficult since then. It is not the same business at all. Now we are bad guys. And it's become too dangerous."

He touched at the blackened lens before he glanced up at Tree and said, "You appear lost, my friend."

Tree said. "Yeah? Do you think so?" Trying to sound tough. As though he was not the kind of guy you should mess with.

The man seemed unconcerned. "You had better sit beside me. There isn't much room here."

"Thanks," Tree said. A thin beard covered the man's gaunt, pale face, and gray hair flowed to his shoulders. Uncertain light glinted off that black lens as he watched Tree seat himself

"What's your name?" the man asked.

"Tree Callister."

"I am Jorge Navidad."

The two shook hands and Jorge Navidad said that although he was originally from a small town in Northern Mexico he had resided in the South Florida area for the past thirty-five years. "Now of course they want to deport me."

"Why do they want to do that?"

Jorge smiled. "They appear to think I sell drugs. I tell them this is nonsense. How could I do such a thing? But they don't appear to believe me. What about you?"

"A cop beat me up and put me in the hospital. Then they charged me with assaulting a police officer."

"So you have not been here before?"

"Actually, the last time I was in here, I was charged with murder."

Jorge's eyes narrowed, as if he was looking at Tree in a different way. He said, "So you are a very dangerous hombre."

"You could say that, but it wouldn't be very accurate."

"No? And how is it you've been misrepresented?"

"I didn't kill anyone. I didn't even assault the police officer."

Jorge grinned. "You see? We are all innocent men here. It is a jail filled with the innocent and wrongly accused. Just ask any of these men."

Tree surveyed the milling inmates, mostly black and Hispanic, everyone in red jump suits, everyone decked out in tattoos.

"But nonetheless," Jorge continued, "here you are, a man of a certain age, a seemingly intelligent fellow."

"You might get an argument about that," Tree said.

"But somehow you end up among these thieves and addicts and murderers, pimps and drug dealers—the worst of the worst. How did you ever get yourself in such a mess?"

"My wife asks me that same question," Tree replied. "I'm not sure how to answer her, either. What's more, when I get out, I've got worse problems to deal with."

"What is worse than being in jail?"

"A woman who threatens to kill me."

"A woman, you say. Dios mío! You live dangerously, my friend."

"Even her friends call her a witch," Tree said.

"La bruja," Jorge said. "La Bruja Mala?"

"A tiny woman. With a face like an axe," Tree said.

"And the name of this witch?"

"I doubt you would know her."

"Try me," Jorge said.

"She goes by the name of Paola. A fearsome woman let me tell you."

Jorge said quietly, "Paola—la Bruja Mala."

"Come on, Tree said. "Don't tell me you know her."

Jorge said, "Stay right here. I will return in a moment."

Jorge rose from the bench and disappeared into the crowd of inmates. Minutes passed, long enough for Tree to start thinking Jorge wasn't returning. He finally reappeared accompanied by a hip hop fireplug with a scraggly beard and a chain of tattooed stars around his thick neck.

The fireplug with the star tattoos looked Tree over before he abruptly slammed him hard against the wall. "Who are you man? What you doing here?"

Jorge whispered something in Spanish into the guy's ear. The fireplug relaxed a bit. "Jorge says you're okay, and maybe you are." He surveyed Tree up and down. "Paola, she never gonna have anything to do with a *pendejo* like you, anyway."

Jorge said, "It's like I tell you, Che, she wants him dead."

"That's impossible," the guy named Che said. "Paola don't *try* to kill no one. She want to kill you, she *kill* you, and that's the end of it."

"Who is she?" Tree demanded. "Who is this woman?"

Che eyed Tree suspiciously. "You don't know who she is?"

Tree shook his head. Jorge spoke to Che: "Tell him, my friend. Tell him what you know."

"I know what everyone knows," Che said. "She is Paola Ramos. Her old man used to run the Estrella Cartel. When he got himself killed, Paola took over the business. She is such a bad ass, man, much worse than her father."

"Paola runs a drug cartel?" Tree in disbelieving voice.

"Why do you think they call her la Bruja Mala, The Wicked Witch? You on her bad side man, you might as well start digging your grave, because you gonna be in that hole sooner than later."

"There must be something he can do," Jorge said.

"He can kill himself," Che said. "That's what I would do. It would be a much more peaceful death, that's for certain."

"What about a black iris?" Tree said.

"A black iris? What about it?" Che said.

"When Paola kills someone does she leave an iris as a kind of calling card?"

Che shook his head. "I know what you mean, man, but that's not Paola. She kill you, she kill you. She don't waste no money on flowers."

The door at the other end of the holding cell opened and a guard stepped into view amid a chorus of howls and whistles. The guard's voice rose above the din: "Callister. Walter Tremain Callister."

"Here," Tree called out.

"You've got a visitor, Walter. Come along with me."

"You see? There may be hope for you yet," Jorge said a smile.

"I appreciate your help," Tree said.

"Go carefully, my friend."

When Tree shook Che's hand, the inmate said, "Every step you take, hombre. Look over your shoulder. You have made a terrible enemy."

The guard called, "Walter, let's go."

As Tree started away, Jorge grabbed his arm. "There is one thing."

Jorge motioned for Tree to bend closer and when he did, the old man whispered, "Patricio."

"Patricio?"

"Talk to him."

Jorge produced a small, wire bound notebook and tore a page out. He found a ballpoint pen in his pocket, and then positioned the paper on the cover of the notebook and wrote down a number. He handed it to Tree.

"Tell him you come from his old friend, Navidad."

30

Tree followed the guard along a series of anonymous passageways twisting through the bowels of the jail. When they came to a door, the guard said, "Here we are."

He opened the door and ushered Tree inside a grim gray room, empty except for metal benches with perforated metal backs facing a flat screen television bolted to the wall. The guard closed the door. Tree was alone.

But only for a moment.

The door opened again and a young Asian man in a dark suit came through. He carried a shopping bag, and he looked very familiar.

"Mr. Callister," the young man said. "I'm not sure if you remember me."

"FBI Special Agent Shawn Lazenby."

"You do remember," Lazenby said with a grin.

Of course he remembered. Lazenby played a small part in Tree's first case on the island, a case involving Tree's former Chicago girlfriend, FBI Special Agent Savannah Trask. It turned out Lazenby was in love with Savannah willing to put his career on the line for her. She had ended up dead, leaving Shawn Lazenby with a broken heart, his career possibly ruined. It had been too late for Tree. Savannah had broken his heart many years before.

Lazenby had aged a bit since his last encounter with Tree. There was a touch of gray at the temples of hair that wasn't as spikey as Tree remembered. Overall, though, Lazenby remained the picture of the efficient, smartly-dressed federal agent.

"Are you still in Miami?" Tree asked.

"Yes sir," Lazenby said.

"The last time I saw you, Special Agent Lazenby, you expressed some doubt as to whether you would continue with the Bureau."

"Yes, well, that worked itself out, and I decided to stay. It was the right decision, I believe. The Bureau has been very good to me."

"So then what brings you back to Fort Myers?"

"Why don't we sit down, Mr. Callister?"

Tree took a seat on one of the wire benches. It wasn't very comfortable, but then it probably wasn't designed to be comfortable. Nothing inside the Lee County jail was. Lazenby unbuttoned his suit jacket and seated himself beside Tree, folding one leg over the other.

"I gotta tell you, Mr. Callister, I wasn't expecting to meet up with you again, and if we did meet, the last thing I expected was to see you in a prison jump suit."

"Are you here because you can do something about that, Special Agent Lazenby? Or are you here to make sure I keep the jump suit?"

"Please, call me Shawn."

"All right, Shawn. Which is it?"

Lazenby lifted up the shopping bag he had brought in with him and placed it on the bench between them. "Your clothes are in here. You can change in this room and then we can walk out together."

"What does that mean?"

"It means the local police have agreed to drop the charges against you, although from what I can see they wouldn't stand much of chance in court, anyway."

"No," Tree said. "I don't think they would."

"Still, they could make it pretty rough on you for the next little while. This way you immediately get released."

"And what do I have to do in exchange for this unexpected generosity?"

"That's the thing, Mr. Callister."

"You can call me Tree, Shawn."

"That's the thing, Tree. You don't have to do anything. In fact, by doing nothing, by dropping your involvement in this case, you would be helping me and the Bureau immensely."

"And how would it help the FBI?"

Lazenby allowed another smile. "I can't say a whole lot more at this point."

"Does this have something to do with a woman named Paola Ramos, the head of the Estrella Cartel?"

Lazenby tried to hide the look of surprise, but couldn't quite pull it off. He sat up straighter and said, "I have no idea, Tree. Besides, what difference does it make, as long as by standing down from all this, it gets you out of jail?"

"It matters because Paola Ramos has threatened to kill me and my wife. I'm told by my new pals here at the Lee County jail that she is the type who will not stop until she succeeds."

"We will take steps to ensure your safety," Lazenby said in a formal voice.

"That's not very comforting, Shawn."

"What choice do you have? If you stay in here, you're a sitting duck. This place is full of people who would cheerfully kill you for a pack of cigarettes. At least outside, we can protect you. There's something else you should consider as well."

"What's that, Shawn?"

"I've already talked to my superiors about this. In exchange for your co-operation, the Bureau is willing to drop the matter of nine million dollars the Tajikistan government claims has been defrauded from them, money you have been accused of having in your possession."

"Shawn, do you really think I'm holding onto nine million dollars?"

"Put it this way, Tree. There are a surprisingly large number of people who do—including the local police. I've had an opportunity to study your activities since the last time we met and frankly there are things you've been up to that, to say the least, raise questions."

"Apparently," Tree said.

"Whatever the truth, I think it's in your best interest if it goes away. You don't need us breathing down your neck, and the FBI has better things to do than waste time trying to catch you with nine million dollars you probably don't have, anyway."

"What about Ryde Bodie?"

"What about him?"

"What's his role in all this?"

"Again, Tree, you're asking me to give you information I can't provide."

"Except I've got his kids staying with me."

"I've arranged for them to be taken off your hands."

"Oh? And what is it, exactly, that you plan to do with them?"

"They'll be protected and well taken care of."

"Ryde or Wayne Granger was working for Wally Garrison, wasn't he? That's how he's involved in this. When Wally died, he and Bonnie tried to run WGE and that's when they messed up with Paola Ramos and the Estrella Cartel."

"Whatever you have figured out, or think you've figured out, makes no difference at this point. What will make a difference is you standing aside and letting us bring this investigation to a successful conclusion. That way, we can ensure your safety, the safety of your family, and of those children."

"I hope you're right," Tree said.

Shawn Lazenby smiled and said, "You don't have to worry about a thing, Tree."

A sure sign to Tree that he had plenty to worry about.

Lazenby stood and handed the shopping bag to Tree. "Why don't you change and then I'll drive you home."

Tree took the bag and Lazenby said, "I'll wait outside."

He got as far as the door before turning and asking the question Tree had been expecting—and dreading. "Do you ever think about her?"

"Who?" As though Tree didn't know.

"You know. Savannah. Savannah Trask."

"I think a lot about the things in my life that failed, about missed opportunities, about what I would do over again in hopes of getting it right this time—so yes, I think about Savannah. What about you, Shawn?"

"I'm married now," Lazenby said. "My wife's a lawyer, although at the moment she's on maternity leave. We have a daughter, five months old."

"Good for you, Shawn—but that doesn't answer the question."

He gave Tree the ghost of a smile. "Come on out when you're finished dressing."

31

When Freddie saw Tree come through the front door, her mouth made a small O of surprise, and she said, "How did you get out?"

"Courtesy of the FBI," he said.

"You look awful," she said, just before she flew into his arms and gently hugged him so as not to cause more pain to his ravaged body.

"You don't think doing jail time gives me a kind of Johnny Cash-outlaw vibe?"

"It makes you look tired and beaten up," Freddie said against his shoulder. "They wouldn't even let me see you in the hospital."

"Back then I was a dangerous, wanted felon," he said.

"What are you now?"

"An innocent man, wrongly accused, a friend of the government."

"I can't keep up with all this," Freddie said. "I really can't."

"That makes two of us," Tree said.

Still, she was willing to forgive him—at least for a moment or two—just glad to have him back in a house that was curiously quiet. What was he missing? The kids, she said. The FBI had arrived with a court order allowing two female agents and a local social worker to take away Madison and Joshua. For their protection, they said.

Marcello's foster mother had shown up about five o'clock to collect the protesting boy, reminding him that he was not, despite his insistence, a Sanibel Sunset detective, but a middle school student who had classes to attend. As for Tommy, he had driven off shortly after the kids departed, the unlikely Pied Piper without his followers, made miserable by the loss.

That left Freddie alone, fretting about her imprisoned husband. She kissed him some more and snuggled gingerly against him, restraining her anger at his endless ability to get himself deeper and deeper into trouble he had more and more difficulty getting out of.

"This time I really am through with it," Tree insisted. "All I have to do is mind my own business and stay away from Ryde Bodie and whatever he is up to with this Mexican drug cartel."

Freddie blinked a couple of times and said, "Mexican drug cartel? There's a Mexican drug cartel here?"

"Paola runs it," he said. "Everyone is scared of her. They call her la Bruja Mala, the Ugly Witch."

"Tree," she said grimly. "What have you gotten us involved in?"

"Wally Garrison and his wife Bonnie were selling and reselling car contracts they didn't have through a company called WGE International," Tree explained. "Ryde was involved, too. Somehow, Paola Ramos and her group came into it, and that's when trouble started."

"What kind of trouble?"

"I don't know for certain, but I'm willing to bet the cartel was laundering money through WGE. It probably looked like a great deal to Wally—until it came time to pay off. When Wally died of a heart attack, the cartel went after Bonnie and Ryde Bodie."

"And in the meantime, Ryde's children, not knowing what their father was up to, came to you for help."

"Well, first of all they went to Marcello who brought them to me."

"And now the FBI is involved?"

"Led by my old friend Shawn Lazenby."

"You're kidding," Freddie said. "I thought he left the Bureau."

"He somehow managed to stay in. He's the one who got me released from the Lee County Jail. My guess is the FBI is after Paola and her gang, and stumbled across what she was up to with Wally Garrison. They don't want me poking my nose around, and they know the assault charges are bogus, so it was easy to offer me a deal: a get-out-of-jail free card in exchange for me staying out of their hair. Also, there is another incentive."

"What's that?"

"Special Agent Lazenby promises the FBI will stop listening to all those whispers about the nine million dollars I'm supposed to have."

"Which you don't have," Freddie said.

"Which Paola Ramos nevertheless thinks I do," Tree said.

Freddie looked at him a long beat before she said, "What would make her think that?"

"Ryde might have had something to do with it."

"Good grief," she said.

"But the FBI says it can protect us," Tree said.

"Against a Mexican drug cartel?" Freddie began pulling away from him. "That sounds like we may be in bigger trouble than ever."

"I wouldn't look at it quite that way," Tree said.

"It's those three words: Mexican. Drug. Cartel. They leave you with a sense there is no other way to look at it."

"I'm going to take care of this," Tree said.

"That's not exactly reassuring," Freddie said.

He wrapped his arm around her, as if that might give her more confidence that everything was going to be all right.

It didn't work.

―――――――

They were getting ready for bed when the house phone rang. He picked it up and a voice said, "Hey, buddy, it's me. Just checking in."

Ryde Bodie.

"Where are you?"

"Just wanted to make sure you are okay—and the kids, too."

"The FBI has Madison and Joshua," Tree said. "Agents came for them this afternoon."

To his surprise, Ryde actually sounded relieved. "That's good. The best thing. That way they'll be protected."

"You know I've been in jail."

"Yeah, I heard. That Markfield really is a jerk, isn't he? Sorry, pal. Really, I am. I didn't mean to get you involved like this."

"For a guy who didn't mean to get me involved, you certainly got me involved," Tree said.

"You should have said no to the kids, Tree," Ryde said. "That's all you had to do, and your life would have gone on as it always has. But you couldn't say it, you couldn't say no, and here we are. You and I both made choices, buddy. Now we've got to do our best to make sure those choices don't kill us."

"We need to talk, Ryde."

"We will, buddy, I promise. We will get to all this stuff. But not right now. Right now, I've got other priorities. I just wanted to phone and make sure you're okay—and tell you they've moved up the date of our meeting."

"What do you mean they've moved it up?"

"No big deal. We'll get together tomorrow night and conclude our arrangement."

"I can't do that, Ryde."

There was a pause before Ryde said, "Why not?"

"The FBI made me promise not to get involved."

There was another moment of silence before Ryde said in a tense voice. "Don't let me down, buddy. Please. I'm counting on you. For all our sakes."

The line went dead.

32

The next morning Tree was still so sore from the beating Detective Markfield had administered, that Freddie had to help him out of bed. He couldn't understand it. In action movies, the hero leapt off bridges onto moving trucks. Explosions blew him into the air. Bad guys smashed and kicked at him. Afterwards, the action hero jumped up again and kept going as if nothing happened.

Meanwhile, Tree Callister, the hero of his own action movie, knocked around a bit by an angry cop, and days later he could hardly move.

"It's not fair," Tree said as Freddie helped him take off his pajamas.

"It's called getting old," Freddie said. "Your body is informing you of the obvious: you're no action hero."

"It's my body telling me I need a stunt double."

"At your prices, who would be crazy enough to stand in for you?"

Tree responded with a loud groan as he limped across the room toward the bathroom.

Freddie helped him into the shower where he discovered that he could not lift his left arm higher than his chest, and if he moved his right arm, pain shot through his fractured rib cage. He felt somewhat better after he stood under the hot spray for ten minutes. Freddie helped him into his pants, but he was able to button his shirt without a great deal of teeth-grinding pain.

Freddie went off to work while he struggled in the kitchen with a cup of coffee. He called Rex Baxter. "I didn't know whether you were alive or dead," Rex said.

"What was your preference?"

"I just wish you would quit finding dead bodies on Sanibel," Rex said. "I liked Bonnie. It's a shame what happened."

"I spent the night in jail because of it."

"You're a suspect, I hear."

"What did you hear?"

"Just that you're the one who found her, and that you somehow got yourself arrested—again. What is it about you and jail?"

"You meet a different class of people, no question," Tree said. "There are not a lot of tourists in the Lee County Jail."

"That's because you've driven them all away," Rex said. "Where are you now?"

"I'm at home with every bone in my body aching. I've been ordered to lie low."

"Who ordered you to do that?"

"The FBI."

"What the blazes have you got yourself into this time?"

"You don't know the half of it," Tree said.

"Which is probably just as well. At the risk of saying something I might regret for the rest of my life—is there anything I can do?"

"Make sure I get a proper burial if it comes to that."

"That's provided there's anything left of you to bury."

"Also, you don't know where I can find Ryde Bodie by any chance?"

"All I know is that everyone seems to be looking for him, particularly after Bonnie's death."

"Tell me again how he got involved in the Oscar show at Big Arts."

"He came into Dayton's, like I told you before," Rex said. "He was with Bonnie. She introduced him. Ryde said he had just moved to the island. He said he wanted to get to know people. Bonnie said he was a real character and thought he would be a great addition to the show—which he turned out to be, incidentally."

Unspoken thought: *Unlike some other people I know.*

"He also wanted to meet you," Rex added.

"He wanted to meet me?"

"He asked if it was true we had a private detective on the island. I had to admit that was the case, although many of us wonder about him."

"Did he suggest we be in the skit together?"

"I don't know," Rex said. "He might have. I can't recall. What difference does it make?"

"Tell me this," Tree said. "Did you say anything to him about the nine million dollars I'm supposed to have?"

Rex paused before he said, "I didn't say anything."

"It's no big deal," Tree lied.

"It may or may not be a big deal," Rex said. "But I didn't tell him."

"Okay," Tree said.

"You know, it's not exactly a secret around the island."

"Isn't it?"

"No, it isn't." Rex sounded adamant.

"Don't worry about it. I'll talk to you later."

"Are you coming into the office?"

"No," Tree said.

"That doesn't sound like you're doing what you're supposed to do," Rex said.

"What am I supposed to do?"

"You're supposed to do nothing, aren't you?"

And that's what he was going to do, Tree thought as he sipped his coffee after hanging up the phone.

Nothing.

That's what he was going to do.

So if Rex did happen to mention to Ryde Bodie that a private detective on Sanibel Island, an ex-newspaperman who everyone thought was crazy to have become a detective in the first place, could be hiding nine million dollars, then a guy like Ryde, in trouble with a Mexican drug cartel, might conclude that if he played his cards right with that detective, he just might have found a way out of the trouble he was in. He might arrange to be in a skit with the detective at the Big Arts Center. He might even hire that detective in order to get closer to him. He might even invite the vicious head of the drug cartel to dinner so she could meet the detective with the nine million dollars.

Yes, that could be it all right. But even knowing all that, he wasn't going to do anything, because that's what he had promised Special Agent Shawn Lazenby. He was just going to stay out of this and let the proper authorities take care of things.

Except, maybe, he might make one phone call—a call that in all likelihood would amount to, well, nothing. But he would make it, anyway. In his wallet he found the piece of note paper upon which Jorge Navidad, his Lee County jail pal, had scrawled a number.

Patricio.

What could this guy do for him? Not anything, probably.

But…

Tree opened his cell and poked out the number on the key pad. It rang three times before someone picked up. The person who answered did not say anything, but Tree could hear the sound of breathing.

Tree said, "Hello?"

The voice on the other end said, "Yes?"

"Is this Patricio?"

"Who is this?"

"My name is Tree Callister. I'm a friend of Jorge Navidad. He suggested I give you a call."

Whoever was on the other end of the line remained silent.

"Patricio?"

"There is no one here by that name."

Then the person on the other end hung up.

Tree finished his coffee and then decided to walk to the beach, in hopes that by keeping his joints moving, relief might come to his many aching parts. The surf walkers were out, ancient mostly, lumbering along the ocean's edge, bellies protruding over shorts and bathing suits, shirts flapping in the breeze, dark glasses reflecting the sunlight that would soon heat the beach to furnace-like temperatures. They moved stork-like, bent forward as if anticipating a strong wind or an unexpected blow, determined, Tree mused, to live forever. He could not bring himself to join the herd. He felt old enough as it was, without having to be reminded of it. He was deciding to return home when his cellphone rang. He swiped it open.

"Tree, this is FBI Special Agent Shawn Lazenby."

Tree said, "Hello, Shawn."

"I thought we had an agreement," Lazenby said.

"What makes you think we don't?"

"Ryde Bodie's children."

"What about them?"

"Do you know where they are?"

"You said they're with you."

"Well they aren't."

"I'm having trouble following you, Shawn."

"Apparently they have exited the safe house where we were billeting them," Lazenby said in his formal FBI agent voice.

"They exited? What's that mean?"

"It means they have disappeared," Lazenby said, exasperation showing.

"I don't have them," Tree said.

"Supposing we don't believe you, Tree?"

"That's up to you Shawn, but they aren't with me."

"If we came to your house, would you allow us to look around?"

"I'm not at the house," Tree said quickly. "And neither are the kids. Maybe they're with their father."

"They're not with him," Lazenby said.

"How do you know that?"

Lazenby hung up.

Everyone was hanging up on him, Tree thought ruefully.

———

Just squeezing into the driver's seat of the Beetle was an act of teeth-clenching courage. Once he got himself settled more or less comfortably, Tree drove down to the Sanibel Island School and parked in the lot.

And waited.

After ten minutes or so, the bell inside the school rang signifying the freeing of the inmates for lunch. Tree eased himself out of the car, and hobbled around to the vast playground behind the school that encompassed a base-ball diamond and a soccer field. Tree thought he might spot Marcello among the kids kicking a soccer ball around. Instead, he found him shooting hoops inside a covered pavilion. As soon as he saw Tree, Marcello tossed the ball he was holding to another boy and hurried over to Tree.

"Is it true you were in jail?" he asked.

"And good afternoon to you, too, Marcello," Tree said.

"Is it true?"

"Briefly I was in jail, yes."

"Wow. Jail." Marcello looked impressed. "What was it like?"

"Not very pleasant," Tree said. "I don't recommend it. As soon as they realized they had made a mistake, they let me go. Who told you this?"

"I overheard Ms. Stayner on the phone. Talking to a lawyer."

"You shouldn't be listening in on other people's conversations."

"That's what private detectives do, they listen to things they're not supposed to hear." Marcello spoke with unassailable logic.

"The reason I came over here, Marcello, I wanted to ask you about Madi and Josh."

"Madison doesn't like to be called Madi. She wants to be called Madison."

"When did she decide this?"

"After she met Thomas."

"I see. Well, I'll keep that in mind the next time I see Madison and her brother. Have you heard from them?"

Marcello said, "I'm worried about them."

"Why, Marcello?"

"They've been captured by the FBI."

"I wouldn't put it quite that way."

"That's what they think. That's why they ran away."

"So the FBI doesn't have them?"

"No."

"Do you know where they are?"

Marcello hesitated too long before he said, "Not really."

"Look, there are some people who are after their father, that's why the FBI took them. So they could protect them. If they are not with the FBI, Josh and Madi could be in real danger."

"Excuse me, sir." A voice of authority, ringing behind him. Tree turned to see a woman striding toward him. "Sir, what are you doing here?"

"I'm a friend of Marcello's," Tree said.

"That's Mrs. Middleton," Marcello explained. "She's my teacher."

Mrs. Middleton addressed Marcello when she said, "Do you know this man?"

"He's my partner," Marcello said.

Mrs. Middleton addressed Tree. "Are you a guardian of some sort?"

"My partner," Marcello repeated insistently.

"I just need a couple of more minutes with Marcello," Tree said.

"I'm sorry, sir, but you can't be here unless you have a visitor's pass. Do you have a pass?"

"I just wanted to speak to him for a moment."

"Do you have a pass?" More demanding this time.

"No, I don't."

"Then, sir, you have to go to the office, show some identification, and they will provide you with the proper visitor's pass."

Mrs. Middleton, in strict authority figure mode, now turned her attention to Marcello. "Behavior Rewards Day is just about over, Marcello. It's time for you to return to class."

Tree focused on Marcello. "Did Josh and Madison tell you where they are?"

Marcello shook his head. Tree didn't like the look on the boy's face.

"Marcello, do you know where they are?"

"Sir!"

"I'd better get back to class," Marcello said.

"Sir, please. If you don't leave, I will have to call school security."

Mrs. Middleton was pulling out her cellphone.

"I'll be in touch," Tree called as he retreated. He got a final glimpse of Marcello as Ms. Middleton hustled him into the school. Behavior Rewards Day was indeed over.

Tree sat in the parking lot for a few minutes not sure what his next move should be. Not certain there was a next move. The school had become quiet, everyone returning to the serious business of learning. He tried to convince himself that he was going to do exactly what he told Shawn Lazenby he would do—stay out of this.

Sure, that's what he was going to do all right.

Then his cellphone rang.

The voice on the other end of the line said, "Señor Tree Callister?"

"Yes," Tree said. "Who's this?"

"I understand you are looking for Patricio."

33

The low-slung sand-colored warehouse stood on a bleak patch of industrial land just off Martin Luther King Boulevard. Tree parked in front of concrete steps leading to a glass-fronted door. He went through the door into a linoleum-floored lobby area with a counter to the right. No one was in sight.

He was wondering if he was in the right place when a bald-headed man who hadn't shaved for a couple of days, wearing a leather jacket, came through a pair of doors beyond the counter. The guy motioned for him to come through the doors. Tree followed him into a good-sized room, empty except for two more men who also shaved their heads but had not recently shaved their faces. They did not wear leather jackets but they carried lethal-looking semi-automatic weapons. They held guns in a way that suggested they knew how to use them.

Nobody said anything. Tree stood looking at the three shaved-headed men. They looked back at him with tough, expressionless faces. Then someone's ring tone sounded: Carly Rae Jepsen singing "Call Me Maybe." One of the shaved-headed men looked embarrassed. He swiped his phone and said, "Si?" The man listened for a few seconds and then looked at the others and nodded.

That was the signal for the men to open another door. Tree was led into a vast warehouse area filled with granite and marble slabs on big metal racks. A huge slab of marble dangled from a sling attached to an overhead crane. They advanced along one of the rows to another door. One of the men held the door open and motioned for Tree to go through.

Tree found himself inside a much smaller room full of office furniture, the walls adorned with photographs of impressive-looking marble pieces. An old fashioned cathode-ray television was propped on a jagged marble shard. An old man in a wheelchair, frail-looking, with a head of luxurious white hair and a carefully trimmed white beard framing a thin, brown face, gazed at the TV. On the screen, a youthful Elvis, his hair a shiny black hood of perfection, said something in Spanish to an equally perfect, bikini-clad Ursula Andress.

"Elvis in *Fun in Acapulco*," the old man said. "It is, as the title suggests, a movie that takes place in Acapulco. I like it because it is one of the few American movies that does not depict Mexicans as murderous cutthroats. Mind you, Elvis never set foot in Mexico. All his scenes were filmed in Los Angeles."

The old man continued, "Then of course there is the attraction of Elvis's co-star, the lovely Ursula. Was there ever a more beautiful woman in the movies? Not a great actress, I grant you, but dios mío, she has only to appear and she still makes an old man's mouth water."

The white-haired man wore a linen jacket over a collarless white shirt. He turned away from the TV set. In the bluish light thrown off by the screen, Tree saw haunted eyes set deep into his face. The eyes flicked across Tree.

"Elvis was a true original, an artist," the white-haired man said, "but an artist strangely corrupted, I believe, by people who did not understand his art and wanted only to make money from him, and thus destroyed him."

"You are Patricio?"

"Let us presume."

"Other than the unexpected insight into Elvis and his movies, I'm not certain why I'm here."

The old man raised a bony, liver-spotted hand. "Possibly to save your life."

"You know a woman named Paola Ramos?"

Patricio gave a smile as haunted as those deep-set eyes. "It was Paola and her father who put me into this wheelchair. I know her only too well."

"Then you know about the trouble I am in."

"Paola's father was the police chief in a province in Northern Mexico. He fell in with the local narcos. These narcos were not very good, so Paola's father took over and turned the organization into a powerful force dominating the state—that is until his untimely death."

"The father was killed?"

"I'm afraid so," Patricio said.

"Who killed him?"

"If you listen to Paola, she would say it was me."

"I see."

"An act that in retrospect was ill-advised, I admit. Paola's father was much easier to get along with than Paola. After she took over the gang, she proved to be many, many times more ruthless and ambitious than her father ever was.

"For a time the Estrela Cartel under Paola did very well. But now that has begun to change. The efforts of the government to bring down the narcos have taken a particular toll on her business. What's more, she has engaged in endless wars with other gangs so that now she is almost broke and desperate for money."

"Which begins to explain what she is doing in South Florida," Tree said.

"Paola always wants something," Patricio said. "What is it she wants from you?"

"Nine million dollars."

"The question is, do you have it?"

"Supposing I did? What then?"

"If you have it and give it to her, she will kill you, and probably kill your wife as well."

"She says she won't do that."

Patricio shrugged and said, "She is lying. Paola always lies. Particularly when it comes to killing. She kills everyone. That is what she does. She is a killing machine."

Tree found himself having trouble swallowing—a recurring problem when his life was in jeopardy. "So what can I do?"

"There is only one way to stop Paola," Patricio said.

"Do I have to ask what that is?"

"You cut off the head of la Bruja Mala."

"I'm not very good at cutting people's heads off," Tree said.

"Obviously not," said Patricio. "From my perspective, you can imagine I am not happy to discover that you could provide Paola with badly needed operating capital. She must not get her hands on your money."

"So what are you proposing?"

"When are you supposed to meet Paola?"

"Tonight."

"Where?"

"That I don't know yet."

Patricio said, "I suggest you go ahead with the meeting."

"Where will you be?"

"Don't worry about us, Mr. Callister."

"And supposing I don't actually have the money?"

Patricio's eyes appeared to sink even deeper into his lined and creviced face. "Then you had better find the money between now and your rendezvous. Otherwise, Paola will be very unhappy. And so will I."

On the TV set, Tree saw Elvis, poised atop a high cliff, preparing to dive hundreds of feet into a sea strewn with rocky outcroppings. Elvis looked uncharacteristically nervous. Tree knew how he felt.

34

Freddie hadn't arrived home by the time Tree pulled into the drive at Andy Rosse Lane.

He parked the car and went through the house into the darkened garage. He snapped on the wall light, illuminating the interior with its built-in workbench and shiny tool board, both empty and unused, the current male occupant of the house not being much of a home handyman. Not much of anything these days, he reflected, simply an aging man, his body racked with pain, possessed of a boundless ability to get himself into trouble he was not certain he could get himself out of again.

An aging man finding it far too easy to feel sorry for himself.

Tree stopped in the middle of the garage. For a couple of moments he heard nothing. Then, from above, movement. Scrambling back and forth. Whispers. Tree moved forward to where a cord dangled from the trap door in the garage ceiling. He grabbed the cord and gave it a good yank. The trap door dropped down unfolding accordion steps. He climbed the steps into the crawlspace between the ceiling and the slant roof. He heard a gasp.

Marcello, along with Joshua and Madison, sat on the floor, staring at Tree, surrounded by the bundles of cash they had removed from the duffle bags beside them.

Madison said, "We didn't do anything." She held a cash bundle in her tiny hand.

"It's all right," Tree said. "Come on, let's go downstairs."

"Are we in trouble?" Joshua asked. "Marcello told us to stay here."

"That's what I figured." Tree looked at Marcello who stared back defiantly. "This is his favorite hiding place."

"I have to protect my clients," Marcello said.

"The FBI may not agree with you," Tree said.

"Tough," said Marcello.

"Does Mrs. Lake know you're here?"

"She thinks I'm at a friend's house," Marcello said.

Madison indicated the bundles of cash. "This is not our money," she said.

"I know it isn't, Madi."

"Madison," she said. "It's Madison."

"Come on," Tree said. "Let's go in the house."

The three of them followed Tree down the steps into the garage and waited patiently while he went back up and stuffed the cash bundles into the duffle bags and pushed them back into the recesses of the crawlspace. Not that it would do much good if someone came up here looking for them. But for the moment, Tree didn't imagine anyone would be doing that.

Once he had closed the trap door again, he led the kids into the kitchen. Madison and Joshua wore shorts and T-shirts and looked as though they could use a bath. But otherwise they seemed fine. They wanted to go to McDonald's. Tree said he didn't think that was a very good idea under the circumstances. He offered to make them chicken sandwiches, an offer they eagerly accepted.

"So what made you run away from the FBI?" Tree asked with studied casualness as he set about cutting the chicken slices for their sandwiches.

"We did not run away," corrected Madison. "We just left."

"We didn't like those people," Joshua added.

"How did they get in touch with you, Marcello?"

"How do you think?" Marcello said. "They called me. We all have cellphones, you know." As if every kid in the world had a cellphone—which, when Tree thought about it, was probably true.

Tree addressed Marcello. "So after I left you at the school, you decided to bring them here."

"They were already here," Marcello said.

Joshua nodded. "He said no one would find us."

"How did you get here?"

"How do you think?" Marcello, slightly disdainful. As if everyone should know this stuff. "We took a taxi."

"Okay," Tree said to Marcello. "But why didn't you tell me what you're doing? I thought we are partners."

"We're only partners when it suits you," Marcello said.

"Besides, you're an adult." Madison made it sound as though that was not a good thing.

"And you would take us back to those people we don't like," Joshua added.

"You're not going to make us go back, are you?" Madison asked in a worried voice.

"I'm going to make you a chicken sandwich," Tree said.

"That's not answering the question." Marcello, adamant. "My clients have a right to know what's in store for them."

"They're my clients, too, Marcello," Tree said.

"I wonder about that," Marcello said.

"If I was going to turn them in, I wouldn't bother making sandwiches," Tree said.

The two children looked relieved. Despite himself, so did Marcello.

"Would you like lettuce and tomato?"

"I don't like tomatoes," Madison said.

"I don't like lettuce," Joshua said.

"I don't want a sandwich," Marcello said.

"What do you want?"

"I'm not hungry," Marcello answered. He was trying to be adult, Tree surmised. Marcello apparently had decided adults would not eat at a time like this.

Tree said to Joshua and Madison, "What about the two of you? Do you want mayonnaise?"

They both agreed to mayonnaise. Tree got a jar from the refrigerator, spread mayonnaise on the seven-grain bread Freddie had brought home the day before. Presented with the chicken sandwiches, Joshua immediately grabbed his and tore into it, a young wolf at feeding time. Madison, by contrast, was the suspicious gazelle, inspecting her food carefully, wily enough not to dive into anything as potentially dangerous as a sandwich before thoroughly checking it out.

Tree said to Joshua, "Can I see your cellphone?"

Marcello frowned. "Why would you want to see his cellphone? Why wouldn't you want to see mine?"

"Because I thought there would be less of an argument if I asked to see Josh's."

"You can look at mine," Madison said.

"I don't know if this is a good idea," Marcello said.

Nonetheless, Madison fished into her pocket and brought out a small pink device she presented to Tree. "There," she said.

A Samsung Galaxy wrapped in a protective case. Tree swiped it open and went to contacts. There weren't many, and nothing listed for Ryder Bodie or Wayne Granger. However, there was a listing for WGE International. Tree pressed it. A local number came up.

"What are you doing?" Madison demanded.

"Seeing how it works," Tree said.

"No, you're not," Madison said angrily. "That's my phone. I want it back."

"In a minute," Tree said.

"Stop it!" Madison's little voice rose to a shriek.

"What's wrong?" Marcello demanded. He looked confused.

Tree put the phone to his ear.

Madison screamed.

The phone emitted a fuzzy electronic ring.

Madison yelled, "I want my phone back!" Marcello was on his feet, unsure what he should do.

The phone, ringing. Now Joshua began to look agitated. "You're not supposed to do that," he said.

Then the phone stopped ringing. Ryde Bodie said, "Hello?"

"It's me," Tree said.

"There you are, buddy. How'd you get this phone?"

"The kids are with me."

Ryde said, "That's good. That's perfect."

"Where are you?" Tree said.

"The Santini marina. Looking forward to seeing you. Oh, and Tree, do me a favor. Bring the kids along when you come—and don't forget the money. Otherwise, we're both dead men."

35

Beneath a nearly-full moon, the heavy traffic streaming onto Fort Myers Beach delayed Tree crossing San Carlos Bridge. Marcello sat beside Tree. The kids, strapped in the backseat, occupied themselves playing Angry Birds on Freddie's iPad. On the radio, Elvis sang "A Big Hunk O' Love."

Marcello frowned at the radio. "What's with this guy? He's supposed to be dead, isn't he?"

"Gone but not forgotten," Tree said.

Marcello grimaced. "Old white dude singing to old white dudes. I gotta get ear plugs when I'm in this car, man. It's embarrassing."

Tree crested the bridge. Pinpoints of light were displayed against the darkness of the bay. Times Square and Estero Boulevard were a distant glimmer.

Was it bad parenting to bring the children along? Undoubtedly. But what choice did he have? Turn up with the money and the kids, Ryde said. Also, he didn't want to leave them behind in case the police or the FBI arrived at the door. He knew plenty about bad parenting and the stupid decisions that go along with it; he was something of an expert on the subject. Certainly he was nobody's role model tonight.

He swung the Beetle past the tourists streaming across Estero bound for the restaurants along Times Square. A band murdered a Credence Clearwater Revival song on the gazebo near the pier. Throngs swarmed either side of Estero, and the traffic was bumper to bumper. Tree strained around to Madison and Joshua, engrossed in Angry Birds. "How are you guys doing?"

No response. "Josh and Madi?"

"It's Madison," she called back. "I already told you, I don't want to be called Madi anymore."

"Okay, Madison."

"We're on level three," she said distractedly. "There's no sardine can on this version."

"No sardine can?" Marcello sounded incredulous. "You gotta be kidding me."

"It's true," Joshua said. "You launch the sardines and that brings out the eagle, but you can't do it on this."

"Why isn't it there?" Tree asked.

"Because you have to *pay* for that, silly," Madison announced, dismissively, as if everyone in the world should know that you have to pay for the sardine can that launches the eagle.

Marcello, huddled against the door, glanced at Tree. "You sure you know what you're doing, man?"

Tree wasn't at all certain. But he wasn't going to tell Marcello that. "Just sit tight," he said. "It's not far now."

"What's not far? Where are we going, anyway?"

"If you're going to be my partner," Tree said. "You've got to learn not to ask so many questions."

"I don't know," Marcello said. "I'm beginning to wonder about this partner thing."

The traffic began to thin, the bright lights and the crowds swallowed by the night. Tree picked up speed as he came along Estero to the Santini Marina Plaza, outlined in salmon hues.

Tree turned into the parking lot and brought the Beetle to a stop not far from Unit Five, the former headquarters of WGE International. He turned the motor off and swung around so that he faced Marcello with an eye on

Madison and Joshua. They barely acknowledged his presence, so engrossed were they with Angry Birds.

"Okay everyone, I want you to listen to me for a moment." Tree in stern *pater familias* voice, the voice his children had resolutely ignored. But he had Marcello's attention, and even Madison and Joshua raised their heads from the iPad.

"I have to go off for a few minutes, and I want to make sure the three of you stay right here."

"I should go with you," Marcello asserted.

"No you shouldn't, that's the last thing you should do." Tree focused sternly on Marcello. "It's important you stay with Joshua and Madi."

"*Madison*! How many times do I have to tell you?" Angry from the back seat.

"Sorry. Madison. But I want everyone to remain here until I get back."

Madison said, "Can we keep playing our game?"

"Yes, of course. But I don't want you to leave the car, okay?" Tree looked at Marcello. "For once, I need you to do as you're told, Marcello."

"I'm not so good at that," he said.

"I know. But these are your clients. You need to stay here with them. I'll come back for you as soon as I can."

"Are you going to be okay?" Marcello concerned.

"I'll be fine."

"Just…be careful, know what I mean?"

"Don't worry about me," Tree said.

"Yeah, right," Marcello said as he rolled his eyes.

Tree got out and opened the Beetle's trunk to withdraw the two duffle bags. He lugged the bags across the parking lot. Through the skeletal outline of the boat storage units, Tree could make out *el Trueno*. He went down the roadway running behind the mall until he reached the rear of Unit Five and the rusting garbage bin that stood next to the unit's backdoor. He opened the lid and dropped the duffle bags inside.

That done, he made his way back toward the parking lot. Someone came at him out of the shadows. He jerked back in alarm. In the moonlight, Tommy Dobbs' strained, pale face took on an ominous quality.

Tree said, "Tommy, for God's sake." Breathing a sigh of relief.

"Sorry, Mr. C, I didn't mean to startle you."

"I just about had a heart attack. What are you doing here?"

"You keep asking me that question, Mr. C. And I keep giving you the same answer."

"Remind me again what it is."

"Following you."

"And I keep telling you not to follow me."

"And I guess I just don't listen very well."

"No, you don't."

"So what are you doing back here?"

"That's a very good question, and if I had a good answer, I might be inclined to share it with you. But as it is, I don't have a good answer, and so I can't tell you one damned thing, except I need you to leave. Now."

"Can't do that, Mr. C."

"I'm starting to lose patience with you, Tommy," Tree said.

"It's Thomas, Mr. C. How many times do I have to remind you?"

"Look, right now I don't have time for any of this," Tree said, trying to keep the anger out of his voice, failing.

"I think you're in trouble, and you need help."

"I'm always in trouble. It's my default position in life these days. There's nothing you can do to help except get yourself in trouble, too."

"I'm not going anywhere."

Tree groaned and then had a thought: "You really want to help?"

"Why do you think I followed you?"

"Because you're under the illusion there's a story."

"Yes, well, that, too. But I want to help."

"You know where I parked the car?"

"I followed you from the house, so yeah, I know."

"Okay, the kids are with me."

"I know," Tommy said. "I saw you put them in the car. I couldn't believe it."

"I didn't have much choice," Tree said. "I want you to stay with them until I come back."

"What happens if you don't come back?"

"I'm coming back," Tree asserted. "But in case I don't, drive away and call Special FBI Agent Shawn Lazenby. Here's my key and here's his number." He handed Tommy the car keys and Lazenby's business card.

"I'm not sure what you're up to Mr. C. But I take it you've got a gun with you."

"I don't like guns."

"You're kidding me."

"Listen, I'll be fine. Just go back to the car and stay with the kids."

Tommy opened his jacket. Tree saw the gun stuck in Tommy's belt. "What's that?"

"It's a gun, Mr. C."

"What are you doing with a gun?"

"Are you kidding? Everyone's got one."

"I don't."

Tommy pulled the gun from his belt and handed it to Tree. "Now you do."

Tree looked at the gun in his hand. Tommy patted him on the arm. "Welcome to South Florida, Mr. C."

36

Tree stood at edge of the dock holding the gun. Then he jammed it into his pocket and went up the gangplank and stepped onto *el Trueno's* aft deck. Ryde Bodie sat cross-legged, lighting a cigarette.

"I didn't know you smoked," Tree said.

Ryde tried on a wry smile through a haze of cigarette smoke. "I didn't for twenty years—until I met you, Tree."

"Life was certainly quieter before I met you, Ryde," Tree said.

"So you've got the kids."

Tree nodded. "They're waiting in the parking lot."

Ryde seemed agitated as he blew cigarette smoke into the night air. "You really did bring them with you, huh? You know what I was thinking? I was thinking that maybe, just maybe, you wouldn't and that would be one less problem to deal with. But then I don't think you're very smart, are you, Tree?"

"Maybe you're right, Ryde. Maybe I'm as dumb as they come. But look at the company I'm keeping—a con man trying to rip off a Mexican drug cartel. How many people have died because of your smart moves? Three people at least, including Bonnie Garrison, who I think you actually cared about."

"You do, do you? You think I cared about Bonnie?" Ryde had progressed from agitated to angry. "Well, maybe I did, although if it wasn't for her I might not have gotten into this mess in the first place."

"Bonnie and Wonderful Wally Garrison."

"Wonderful Wally," Ryde said caustically, blowing more cigarette smoke. "He was wonderful all right. In his way, he was even stupider than you, Tree. Messing with Paola and her gang. If I live to be a thousand—which given our current circumstances I doubt is going to happen—I will never understand what he was thinking."

"The Ponzi scheme that couldn't help but fail," Tree said.

"Ponzi scheme." Ryde made a face and flicked ashes on the deck. "Everything's a Ponzi scheme when it comes down to it. The world runs on Ponzi schemes. How do you think banks operate? Biggest Ponzi scheme of them all. We weren't doing anything any other financial institution doesn't do every day."

"Except when it came time to pay out, Wally couldn't do it. That's why you've got Paola Ramos on your back threatening to kill us all."

"Hey," Ryde said, brightening, "I was smart enough to figure you for what you really are."

"You don't know anything about me, Ryde."

"Sure I do," Ryde said, nodding through a stream of smoke. "You're a guy who stays squeaky clean right up to the moment when he has a chance to get dirty, just like the rest of us. Nine million dollars was the opportunity you couldn't resist."

"You think so?"

"It's human nature," Ryde said. "You didn't have the intestinal fortitude to stand up in front of an audience at the Big Arts Center. That's when I knew for sure you had the money. That's when I knew you couldn't have resisted the temptation. You had the nine million dollars. All I had to do was get it out of you."

He tossed what was left of his cigarette overboard. "I presume you brought it with you."

"What about Paola? Is she here?"

"Waiting inside." Ryde got to his feet. "Come on, you can see for yourself." Seemingly as an afterthought, he said, "That gun."

"What gun?" Tree said.

"The one in your pocket. Maybe it's not such a good idea to go in there with it."

"No?"

"Maybe you better give it to me."

Tree fished out the gun. Ryde took it from his hand. With a disdainful shake of his head, he dropped the gun onto the seat. "That's better," he said.

He led Tree through the glass door and down the short flight of rosewood stairs into the beautifully appointed sitting room. Paola sat on an easy chair, her head thrown back and slightly to one side. Not far away Manuel lay on his stomach in the pool of blood seeping around a black iris.

Blood and flowers, Tree thought. Far too much blood soaked in flowers.

Patricio was on a sofa across from Paola looking dapper despite the gun he was holding. The two shaved-headed guys stood in the shadows at the back of the room.

Tree said to him, "Tell me why you leave a black iris every time you kill someone. What does that do for you? Make murder seem somehow more romantic? Does it give the killing a certain poetry it would lack otherwise? Is that it?"

Patricio just smiled. "I watched the end of *Fun in Acapulco*," he said.

Tree didn't say anything.

"It ended as I imagined, with sunshine and songs, and handsome Elvis going off with the beautiful Ursula and a Mexican kid. Now what are they going to do with the boy? I wonder. They would become his father and mother? This beautiful couple is going to want to deal with some Mexican kid for the rest of their lives?" He shrugged. "Somehow I doubt it.

"But I enjoyed it," he went on. "If only all women were like Ursula. If only real life was like an Elvis Presley movie."

"Unfortunately, real life is littered with dead bodies," Tree nodded at the corpses. "At least it is tonight. Dead bodies and black flowers."

"No small thanks to you, Mr. Callister. You flushed out Paola with the help of our friend Ryde."

"Ryde is your friend?"

That induced Patricio's sardonic smile. "Let's say we have joined forces for our mutual benefit." Then the smile was gone. "Now, Mr. Callister, I must ask you for the money I assume you brought tonight."

"It doesn't look like we're going to need it now," Tree said.

Patricio's face darkened. He did not look quite so frail, and Tree could see the man who would kill two people on a yacht without getting upset about it. "There is still a price for your life, Mr. Callister, and for the life of your friend here. I expect you to pay it."

"Come on, Tree, let's not screw around," Ryde said. His voice sounded strained.

Tree looked at Ryde and then at Patricio. Then he said: "The money's in a dumpster in back of unit five at the mall."

Patricio turned to one of the shaved-headed guys and spoke to him in Spanish. Immediately, the shaved-headed guy left the cabin. Ryde noticeably relaxed. He forced a watery smile. "I knew it," he said to Tree. "I knew you would come through, buddy."

A heavy silence enveloped the cabin. Patricio appeared to be lost in thought while Ryde grew tense again, his left leg jerking up and down. The second shaved-headed guy did not move. Only his eyes shifted restlessly from Tree to Ryde and then to his boss and then back to Tree again.

The first shaved-headed guy returned shortly, carrying the two duffle bags. He placed them on the floor in front of Patricio who studied them closely for a few seconds and then glanced at Tree. "Open them," he ordered.

Tree bent over and unzipped one of the bags and turned it upside down. Bundles of cash tumbled to the floor. Tree opened the second bag, exposing its contents.

"What the hell is that?" Ryde Bodie demanded.

Patricio's face was like the side of a cliff. "What are you up to, Mr. Callister?"

"The nine million, just like I promised," Tree said.

Ryde scooped up three of the bundles and held them out to Tree. "It's not nine million in American dollars."

Tree shook his head. "Tajikistani somoni."

"What?"

"It's the currency of Tajikistan," Tree explained. "The somoni. There's nine million somoni in those bags. Well, close to nine million. I may have miscounted a few so-moni."

Patricio continued to stare at the money. Ryde spoke in a strangled voice. "How much is it worth?"

"It's basically worthless in this country," Tree said. "However, if you ever visit Tajikistan, you'll live like a king."

Ryde dropped the money he was holding to the floor. Patricio raised his eyes until they met Tree's. Then he laughed, a full-bodied up-from-the-gut roar that shook his frail body. "I should kill you," he said. "I should kill the two of you. But I suppose in your curious way, Mr. Callister, you have paid for your life and for the life of Ryde Bodie."

Patricio turned to the shaved-headed guy who had transported the money onboard the yacht and rattled off more Spanish. Immediately, the shaved-headed guy bent over and began gathering up the bundles of cash and replacing them in the duffle bag.

"Help me to my feet, Mr. Callister," Patricio said.

Tree held out his arm, and Patricio used it to pull himself off the sofa. He wobbled and Tree caught him in his arms. He was all skin and bones. It was like holding a skeleton. "I've acquired a DVD of *Tickle Me*," Patricio said, slightly out of breath from the exertion of standing. "Have you seen it?"

"Probably, a long time ago."

"Elvis is referred to as a bronc buster in the movie. Do you know what that means? A bronc buster?"

"It means he's Elvis," Tree said. "No matter who he plays, he is always Elvis."

Patricio grinned and said, "It takes place at a rodeo. I can't wait to see it. How close to a horse do you think he got?"

"About as close as he did to Acapulco in *Fun in Acapulco*."

Patricio laughed and one of the shaved-headed guys came forward so that the old man could switch from Tree's arm to the shaved-headed guy. "You'd better go, Mr. Callister. We'll finish up here."

Ryde said, "What about the money?"

Patricio's eyebrows shot up. "As I said, it is the price of your life, so I will keep it. In my business, you never know, nine million somoni may come in handy one day."

Patricio held out his hand to Tree. "I believe people underestimate you, Mr. Callister. That is the mistake they make."

"There are times when I wonder," Tree said.

"Take it from an old man who has survived in the jungle for a long time—you are worth more than nine million somoni."

They shook hands and Tree went with Ryde back to the aft deck and then onto the dock.

Chuckling, Ryde threw his arm around Tree as they walked toward the roadway. "Well, buddy, I've got to hand it to you. When it comes to chutzpah, you take the cake. When you dumped all that crap currency on the floor, I thought we were both dead men."

Tree moved away from Ryde's enveloping arm. "What I still can't figure, Ryde, is just how you fit into all this. Whose side are you on, anyway?"

"I'm on my side," Ryde said. "I'm like that old man back there, a survivor in the jungle."

"Your kids don't know who you are," Tree said. "And after all this, I'm not sure, either."

"I'm whatever's necessary, Tree. And right now, I'm the guy who's walking away from this thanks to Tree Callister and nine million somoni."

He stopped and looked at his watch. "The trouble is, buddy, I was expecting to walk out of there with nine million real American dollars."

"Sorry about that, Ryde."

"You've let me down." Ryde drew out the gun Tree had given him.

"Maybe I shouldn't have given you the gun," Tree said.

"No, you shouldn't have," Ryde said. He looked at his watch again.

Then a black-haired man was coming towards them.

It was Diego. And he had a gun, too.

37

Diego shouted in Spanish. His gun hand moved in slow motion. Tree had a fleeting moment to think, So this is what it's like just before you die, watching a man point the gun that would kill you.

He was thinking this when the world exploded.

He turned in time to see *el Trueno* lift off its berth in a great fireball that lit up the night. As the yacht rose into the air, its upper decks came apart. Debris began to rain down around them. Diego, having been staggered by the shock wave, now was hit by a flaming missile that set his clothing on fire. He screamed and the gun in his hand went off with a pop all but lost in the noise and the light.

Tree felt as though someone had hit his thigh with a two-by-four. He gasped and sank to the ground. A veil of pain descended. Through the veil, he saw Diego, transformed into a fiery dancer. Ryde was watching, too, still holding Tree's gun. What was left of *el Trueno* continued to burn fiercely, setting the docks ablaze and shooting fireballs into the night sky. Tree focused on Ryde, not moving in the firestorm.

"Looks like you've been shot," Ryde said.

"Yes."

"Well then, maybe I'll just shoot you again."

He pointed the gun at Tree. Tree shook his head to get a better view of Ryde through the smoke and fire.

"You know something, Ryde," Tree said.

"What's that, Tree?"

"From here, it looks as though you really are going to shoot me."

Ryde let Tree have one of his megawatt grins. "What can I tell you, buddy? Maybe you're not as dumb as I thought."

And at that moment, Tree was certain he would take the bullet. Damn, he thought. Life wasn't fair. People kept trying to kill him.

Tree was thinking this when Ryde suddenly went flying forward. Tree glimpsed Marcello, his arms wrapped around Ryde's legs, trying to drag him to the ground.

Ryde fought to maintain his balance with Marcello attached to him as a series of smaller explosions shook the air. Ryde's face twisted into an expression of rage, a moment before Special Agent Shawn Lazenby took over from the struggling Marcello, forcing the gun from Ryde's hand and then wrestling him to the ground.

The next thing Marcello was holding Tree, his face solemn. "Dude," he said. "Can you hear me?"

Dude?

"I can hear you," Tree groaned. "Tell me I haven't been shot."

There were tears in Marcello's eyes. "You've been shot."

"Freddie's going to kill me," Tree said. "She hates it when I get shot."

Marcello said something Tree couldn't understand, and then he saw Madison, saucer-eyed, and Joshua, equally saucer-eyed. Tommy was with them and he was saying something, too, but darned if Tree could make out what it was.

Then FBI Special Agent Lazenby hovered above him. He thought of Freddie, and then he thought of Elvis in *Tickle Me.*

What the hell was a bronc buster, anyway?

38

Tree lay on white satin in an open coffin, his hands folded neatly, holding a black iris. Tree stared at the flower. This was not a good sign, he thought.

Presently, a young man dressed in a cowboy outfit, his black hair perfectly framing a round face thick with what looked like bronze makeup, peered at him over the coffin edge. He said, "We all loved you, sir. Truly."

"Where am I?" Tree asked.

"Son, you're in the living room at Graceland, the home you named after your beloved momma."

"No, no," Tree protested. "You're supposed to be in here, not me."

"Hey, I only shot out a few television screens. You're the one who keeps stopping bullets. You do that often enough, and this is how you end up."

"Why are you dressed like that, anyway?"

"This is the way Lonnie Beale dresses, man. I'm a singing rodeo rider who works at a dude ranch. Except there are no dudes, just a lot of gorgeous chicks anxious to jump on my bones."

"That's the plot for your movie, *Tickle Me*," Tree said.

"Man, the crowds outside the gates, they're unbelievable. Who knew your death would touch so many people."

"I keep having this nightmare, all sorts of smoke and fire around me, and Ryde Bodie about to shoot me."

"That wasn't a nightmare, sir. He *was* gonna shoot you."

"Why would he shoot me?" Tree said.

"You're the detective, sir, you figure it out. The fact is, someone beat him to it. So what Ryde Bodie was going to do or not going to do, doesn't make much difference. Fact is, you're the one in the coffin."

"I can't be dead," Tree said. "I don't want to die."

"Then you shouldn't keep getting shot. Death is the logical outcome of getting shot. That's why they shoot you in the first place."

No," Tree cried. "I don't want to be at Graceland. I don't want to die!"

"There you are," Nurse Lindsay said, coming into focus.

"Am I at Graceland?" Tree Callister asked.

"Where's Graceland?"

"It's in Memphis, Tennessee."

She gave him a quizzical look. "You're in a private room at Lee Memorial. Don't you remember me?"

"Lindsay," Tree said.

She flashed a beatific smile and said, "That's right. And here you are, with us one more time."

"I missed you," Tree said.

"Well, you didn't have to get yourself shot in order to see me again. Neither did Mr. Bodie."

"Is he here?" Tree said.

"Just for observation. He wasn't shot or anything."

"There's something about me that makes people want to shoot me."

"In the scheme of things, that's a pretty minor gunshot wound you've got there," Nurse Lindsay said. "The bullet just grazed your thigh. It didn't shatter any bone and it missed the femoral artery. So in the long run, your walking won't be affected. You should see some of the people who come in here. You're small potatoes, if you don't mind my saying so. Although——" She allowed her voice to trail off.

"Although what?" Tree said.

"We took a little poll last night and decided you're about the oldest gunshot victim we've had. Mostly it's kids shooting one another. Very seldom do we get an older gentleman with a gunshot wound."

"This should be an indication that I'm not an older gentleman," Tree said. "No one shoots old guys."

"Every once in a while someone does," Lindsay corrected.

Marcello poked his head in the room. "This young man was here yesterday, too," Lindsay said. "He's a real little sweetheart."

"I'm not a little sweetheart," Marcello said coming into the room. "I'm his partner—and I saved his life."

"Did you? That's impressive," Nurse Lindsay said. "I'll come back in a little while and check on you, Mr. Callister."

She smiled and made her exit. Marcello wore a blue-striped T-shirt and a pair of baggy shorts that hung down past his knees. He eased himself into the molded plastic chair beside Tree's bed.

"That was very courageous what you did, Marcello," Tree said.

"Mrs. Lake says I shouldn't have done it. I could have been killed."

"She's right about that."

"I saved your life," Marcello repeated proudly.

"That's if Ryde Bodie was really going to shoot me," Tree said.

"He didn't seem to have that gun pointed at anyone else," Marcello said. "Of course, I jumped him and saved your life."

"You keep saying that."

"Because it's true," Marcello asserted.

"Have you seen Madi and Josh?"

"Madison. She doesn't like to be called Madi."

"Yes, I know. Have you seen them?"

"They've gone away."

"Gone away? Where?"

Marcello raised and lowered his shoulders. "They went with their dad."

"I thought he would be in jail."

Marcello fished into his pocket, and brought out a folded piece of notepaper. "Madison wasn't supposed to, but she wrote you a letter. I promised her that I'd make sure you got it." He opened it up and handed it to Tree.

Madison had carefully printed on the lined sheet torn from a wire bound student's notebook. It read:

Dear Mr. Callister

We are going away with our dad. We can't say where. Thanks to you we know what he does. He helps the FBI. Sorry you got shot. Sorry we can't visit you. They won't let us.

Yours very sincerely,

Madison Bodie

At the bottom of the letter, Madison had drawn a flower with black petals.

Marcello said, "That stuff about helping the FBI, is that what he really does?"

"Help me out of bed," Tree said.

"We didn't do a very good job."

Tree threw back the covers and began to ease his wounded leg off the mattress. "What do you mean?"

"They hired us to find out about their father, and they ended up having to find out for themselves. We didn't do anything."

"Well, I would say we gave them a helping hand."

"I wouldn't say that," Marcello said. He got off the chair and allowed Tree to lean on him. "Anyway, I have to get going."

"Just a minute," Tree said. "I need you."

"What are you doing?"

"Just help me, will you?"

"Okay, but Mrs. Lake is waiting. She says as a result of what happened, she doesn't want us to be partners."

Leaning on Marcello, Tree began hobbling toward the door. "No? Why is that?"

"She says it's too dangerous, and I should concentrate on my school work."

"Okay," Tree said.

"I probably should be associated with a better detective, anyway."

"You probably should," Tree said.

"Someone who can get the job done."

They reached the nurse's station. Nurse Lindsay looked up, ballpoint pen poised over the paperwork she was finishing. "You shouldn't be out of bed, Mr. Callister."

"What room is Ryde Bodie in?" Tree said.

"I'm not sure I'm supposed to tell you that," Lindsay said.

"Please," Tree said. "It's very important."

"He's downstairs." She consulted a chart, and then gave him the room number.

Marcello, grumbling, navigated Tree to the elevator. "I don't know what we're doing," he said.

"You're helping me, like a partner should," Tree said.

"Yeah, well, like I said, I don't think we can be partners."

The elevator arrived. Tree eased onto it and leaned against the railing.

"Hey, it's okay," Tree said. "We may not be partners, and I'm probably not much of a detective, but that doesn't mean we can't be friends."

"I did save your life," Marcello said. "That's something, isn't it?"

"It certainly is," Tree said.

"And I helped you onto the elevator."

When they reached the second floor, Tree leaned on Marcello and together they found Ryde's room.

Only the room was empty. A single black iris lay on the bed sheet.

39

Tree picked up the iris, and Marcello said, "How come he leaves a flower behind? What's that all about?"

Before Tree had to come up with an answer, Special Agent Shawn Lazenby entered. "I was just upstairs looking for the two of you," he said. "Marcello, your mom's waiting in the lobby. I think you'd better go meet her."

Marcello looked at Tree. "Sure you're gonna be all right?"

"I'll be fine," Tree said. "Thanks for your help, Marcello."

"We never even got paid," Marcello said.

"No, we didn't," Tree admitted.

Marcello shrugged. "But I guess that's all right, since we came out partners in the end."

Then to Tree's surprise, Marcello hugged him hard before disappearing from the room.

Holding the iris, Tree swallowed a couple of times, and then made himself focus on Lazenby. "It was Ryde," he said.

"It was Ryde what?" replied Lazenby.

"Ryde killed Rodrigo on the yacht. Then he set fire to his own house so he could cover up Jim Waterhouse's murder—and probably collect a hefty insurance payment in the bargain. If he didn't kill Paola and Manuel Ramos himself, he engineered it so that Patricio and his men would do it for him—that is, after Patricio's hit man failed to kill him on Rabbit Road. Once Paola and Manuel were taken care of, he arranged to blow Patricio to hell and gone so he wouldn't have any second thoughts about coming after him."

"I think maybe you're giving Mr. Bodie far too much credit," Lazenby said.

"What I don't understand is why he would kill Bonnie. She wasn't in his way—or was she? Maybe as long as Bonnie was still alive, she could turn on him, and he didn't want that."

"As far as the police are concerned, it was Diego who murdered Mrs. Garrison," Lazenby said.

"And the really amazing thing is, you're protecting him, letting him get away with all this."

"I have no idea what you're talking about," Lazenby said.

"Then where is he? Where is Ryde Bodie or whatever the hell his name is?"

"Don't get your shirt in a knot, Tree," Lazenby said in a warning voice. "You've come out all right."

"Where is he?"

Lazenby sighed and said, "He's in a safe place, and so are his children."

"What did he do? Come to you once he realized Wally and his wife Bonnie had defrauded a Mexican drug cartel?"

"Let's put it this way, we saw an opportunity to take down the Estrella Cartel, and so we met with Mr. Bodie, and he told us what he could bring to the table."

"And you even bagged a second drug lord, the Great Patricio himself."

"Yes," was all Lazenby said.

"Did Ryde mention he was going to kill everyone who got in his way?"

"We would never agree to anything like that," Lazenby said.

"Of course you wouldn't," Tree said. "But Ryde knew that as long as any of them lived, they could potentially come after him, no matter how well the FBI hid him and his family. He also knew there wasn't much you could do to stop him—or maybe I should say there wasn't much you *wanted* to do."

"Like I said before, I believe you are giving Mr. Bodie far too much credit."

"It would all have worked out just fine, except Ryde's kids couldn't figure out what their father was up to, and so they hired Marcello. He came to me, and fool that I am, I allowed him to talk me into getting involved."

"Yes, I'm sorry about that," Lazenby said. "I must say, though, you put yourself needlessly in harm's way."

"Did I? Or did I get some help finding harm's way from the FBI?"

"I'm not following you," Lazenby said.

"I thought it was Rex Baxter who told Ryde about the millions allegedly stolen from the Tajikistan government I was supposed to be hiding," Tree said. "But it wasn't Rex. It was you."

Lazenby smiled and shrugged. "Maybe, just maybe, we underestimated how Mr. Bodie would put that information to use. Mr. Bodie has a remarkable ability to take advantage of everyone." Lazenby looked at his watch. "I'm going to miss my plane back to Miami."

"So that's it? That's the end of it?"

"I've already told you a lot more than I should, Tree."

He held out his hand. Tree just looked at it. "You know he would have killed me, too, if that boy who just left hadn't risked his life and tackled him."

"I don't think that's the case," Lazenby said. "Mr. Bodie says he's quite fond of you."

"I don't think Ryde Bodie likes anyone but himself," Tree said.

Lazenby shrugged. "Look, these things are always messy. They never quite work out the way you hope. But in this case, they did work out, so let's just leave it at that."

"Sure," Tree said. "Why don't we?"

"Hope you're going to be all right." Lazenby didn't sound too concerned one way or the other. Tree could easily imagine him already onto the next case. This one was closed, the dead buried or missing, the survivors hospitalized or in hiding. Time to move on.

"I'll be fine," Tree said.

"I hope so," Lazenby said. "But why do I suspect that a guy like you, Tree, is always going to be in some kind of trouble."

Tree tossed the flower to Lazenby who caught it awkwardly. "What am I supposed to do with this?"

"I don't know," Tree said. "Press it between the pages of your memory book so you don't forget the killer you let go free. Maybe you'll look at it every once in a while, and you won't find yourself so easy to live with."

Lazenby offered a crooked grin. "You take care of yourself, Tree."

When the FBI agent left, he was still holding the black iris.

40

Here's what I don't understand," Freddie Stayner said as her husband leaned on a cane and hobbled across the Lee Memorial Hospital parking lot. Cooler air had overtaken the overnight humidity creating a thickening fog.

"How I could ever manage to get myself shot twice?" interjected Tree.

Actually, once he got the hang of it, the cane was a great aid, and he was sorry he had kicked up a fuss about using it.

"No, that I can understand. Bruce Willis, for example, would know enough to get out of the way of a bullet. You seem to walk right into them."

"Bruce benefits from the fact no one is actually shooting at him," Tree said. "The people I deal with use real bullets."

"All the more reason to be careful," Freddie said.

"What don't you understand?"

"I don't understand why you kept the money in the first place."

"You mean the nine million somonis."

"I think you're making it up," Freddie said. "I don't think there's any such thing as a somoni—unless it's something you eat."

"The one hundred somoni bank note features a very handsome, bearded gentleman wearing a crown."

"Why didn't you just leave the money where you found it?"

"It's funny," Tree said. "You're the first person who's asked me that question."

As they approached Freddie's Mercedes, they saw someone emerge from the fog.

"Tommy Dobbs," Tree said. Trying not to groan when he said it. He should have known. Wherever there was fog or shadow or the darkness of the night, there was Tommy emerging from it.

"*Thomas*, Mr. C."

"Sorry, I've been shot, I'm not myself," Tree said.

"I came around to see you a couple of times, but you were always sleeping," Tommy said.

"I haven't forgotten you, believe me," Tree said. "I suspect you're the one who called in the cavalry."

Tommy seemed pleased to be so acknowledged. "When you didn't come back, and there I was with the kids, and they started to get really restless and tired, I figured I'd better call Special Agent Lazenby."

Tree looked at him. "You *know* Special Agent Lazenby?"

"I talked to him a couple of times for my story."

"What story?"

Tommy grinned. "That's what I wanted to tell you, Mr. C. I heard you were getting out today. The *Sun-Times* loves my piece. They want to talk to me about a possible job on staff. I'm flying to Chicago tomorrow."

"Hold on a minute, Tommy—"

"Thomas."

"You've already *written* a story?"

"The former *Sun-Times* reporter-turned-private-detective, his life saved by a thirteen-year-old boy. Together these two Sanibel Sunset detectives helped bring down a major Mexican drug cartel. It's a heck of a story, Mr. C."

Before Tree could stop him, Tommy embraced him. "I guess I saved your life, Mr. C. But at the same time, you saved my newspaper career. I'll never know how to thank you."

Tree thought there was getting to be quite a line forming of people who claimed to have saved his life.

"You can start to thank me by letting go of me," Tree said. "I'm feeling very fragile at the moment."

Tommy sprang away, looking embarrassed. "Yeah, of course. Sorry, Mr. C."

"Tree," Freddie said in a warning voice. "Be nice. He's done a great job."

Tree looked at his wife. "You've seen the story?"

"It's all over the Internet," Freddie said.

In a more conciliatory voice, Tree said, "Listen I'm glad you've got a shot at a job—Thomas. I'm happy for you. Really, I am. I just wish the story wasn't about me."

"It'll be great for your business, Mr. C," Tommy said enthusiastically. "Just wait and see. Everyone will want to hire the Sanibel Sunset Detective Agency now."

Freddie frowned. "Every time someone hires him, he gets shot."

"It's not *every* time," Tree corrected. "A couple of times, that's all."

"Too many times," Freddie said.

She helped him into the Mercedes. Tommy leaned in the window. "I'll let you know how it goes in Chicago, Mr. C."

"You're joining a dying breed, Thomas, but good luck."

Then Tommy was gone from the window. Tree cleared his throat. Freddie said, "Are you all right?"

"Yeah, I'm fine," Tree said.

"Anything you say, tough guy."

"I don't know whether I mentioned it or not, but I've been shot. Twice."

"I doubt I'm ever going to hear the end of it," Freddie said.

The fog was thicker as Freddie exited the parking lot onto South Cleveland Avenue. Tree said, "You're right."

Freddie glanced over at him. "What am I right about?"

"I should get out of this."

"I never said a thing," Freddie said.

"Yes, but I know what you're thinking."

"I am thinking you should do what your heart tells you—I just wish your heart would tell you to do something that doesn't get you killed."

"My heart is telling me living is better than dying," Tree said.

"Then you should listen to your heart." Freddie brought the car to a stop at Cypress Lake Drive and gave him a quick glance.

"That's what I'm doing," Tree said.

"You're going to give up the Sanibel Sunset Detective Agency?"

"Don't you think it's time?"

When the light turned green, Freddie started the car forward, saying, "If you're asking me, I would say yes. If getting yourself shot a second time isn't a wakeup call, I don't know what is. But that's me, it's not you. You have to do what you think is right for you."

"Lying in that hospital bed, I thought about it a lot," Tree said. "This is what's right for me."

They drove along in silence for a few minutes. Then Freddie said, "You never did answer my question."

"What question was that?"

Freddie's eyes kept darting toward the rear view mirror.

"What's wrong?" Tree said.

"Someone is following us," Freddie said.

41

Tree tried to crane his head around so that he could get a look at who was behind them. But it hurt too much.

"It doesn't look like a police car, but now red lights are flashing," Freddie said, eyes on the rear view mirror.

"Probably an unmarked car," Tree said. "Better pull over."

Freddie slowed, turned into a nearby CVS Drug Store parking lot, and brought the Mercedes to a stop. A brown Buick pulled up beside the car. Two men were in the car. Tree recognized the driver.

"Owen Markfield," he said.

Markfield came over to Freddie's side as she rolled down the window.

Tree said, "You're out of your jurisdiction, aren't you, Detective Markfield?"

"A good police officer is never out of his jurisdiction when he sees wrong being done."

"Exactly what wrong was being done?" Freddie demanded.

Markfield smirked and said, "Other than the fact that you may be transporting a wanted fugitive, you seemed to be going pretty fast."

"I *seemed* to be going pretty fast?"

Markfield looked past Freddie at Tree. "I want you to step out, Callister."

"What's my passenger got to do with the fact I'm supposedly speeding?"

"Tree, don't make me ask you again." Markfield's voice had taken on raspy authority.

"He's just out of the hospital, for heaven's sake," Freddie said. "He can hardly move."

Tree put his hand on Freddie's arm. Her body was tense. "It's all right, Freddie. I'm sure my friend Detective Markfield just wants to wish me a speedy recovery."

"I don't think that's what he wants to wish you," Freddie said.

Tree opened the passenger door as Markfield came around the Mercedes. Straining to extricate himself from the car, it was all Tree could do not to cry out. Leaning hard on his cane he managed to straighten himself so that he was face to face with Markfield.

"You're not armed, are you, Tree?"

"Not me, Detective Markfield."

"Because if I thought you were armed, then I would have every right to shoot you, you being a possible fugitive with a history of gun violence."

"It's all right, Owen, I do not think we have to shoot my friend, Tree."

The second man in the Buick had emerged from the car and now approached Tree and Markfield. Jorge Navidad no longer wore the red jump suit he had on when Tree met him at the Lee County jail—and he no longer wore the glasses with one lens blacked out. He appeared to have two good eyes, and he was clean-shaven now, his shoulder-length hair had been cut back considerably. He wore a blue blazer that complemented nicely-fitting jeans.

"What are you doing out of jail?" was all Tree could think of to say.

"I had to come and see you," Jorge Navidad said with a gentle smile. "One innocent man to another."

"Or maybe you were never really in jail."

"Jorge is an inspector with the Policía Federal Ministerial," Markfield said.

"You're a Federale," Tree said.

"Just a tired policeman anxious to return to his family in Mexico City," Jorge said. "But I couldn't leave without thanking you for your help."

"For being stupid enough to allow myself to be set up?"

"You made the phone call I was hoping you would make," Jorge said. "That made the difference."

He held out his hand. Tree looked at it and said, "You used me."

"I'm afraid we've all been used." Jorge took his hand away. "But what can you do? That's the way it usually works, isn't it?"

"Is it?" Tree said.

Jorge gave the knowing smile of a weary traveler through a duplicitous world. He turned to Markfield. "We had better get to the airport, Owen. I don't want to miss my flight."

"Yeah, I'll be there in a moment, Jorge. I just want to have a final word with Tree."

Jorge Navidad returned to the car. Markfield said to Tree, "I want you to know that whatever has happened or whatever you *think* has happened, it doesn't change anything as far as I'm concerned."

"But you obviously found some use for me," Tree said.

"I think you're a scumbag who's killed a couple of people, so yeah, if I get a chance to throw you to the fishes, I'll do it. You should be dead or in jail. The fact that you are not either of those things is highly disappointing."

Tree worked up a smile and said, "It's always good to see you, Detective Markfield. But I don't think from here on in I'm going to be giving you much reason to put me in prison or shoot me."

"We'll see about that," Markfield said. "We'll just see about that, Callister. I'm still watching you."

He turned and walked back to his car where Jorge Navidad waited.

Tree struggled in beside Freddie, breathing hard from the effort.

She started the car forward. "What was that all about?"

"More evidence to support my suspicion that it's time to retire," Tree said.

———

By the time they approached the burnt-out ruins of the Traven house, the fog had become so thick Freddie could barely see the road in front of her.

Tree asked her to pull over. She parked near the front gates and then helped him out. The gates were closed but not locked. Tree, leaning on his cane, pushed one of them open, and they went through to what was left of the stone façade, a ghost just visible through films of mist.

The roof was gone and the gleaming white porches had been burned away. The upper windows were black eyes staring out at nothing. Sheets of plywood covered the ground floor windows.

However, the stone Great Danes remained intact, flanking the top of the scorched staircase, impassive as always, impervious to the ways of a world far beneath their dignity. Tree, at the bottom of the steps, stared up at the dogs, remembering the times he had trooped past them, his heart in his mouth, wondering what duplicitous hell Elizabeth Traven was about to unleash.

Countless lies had been told inside that house, a few secrets revealed, bodies found. Ryder Bodie had thought he was going to change all that, wipe out the house's dark past, imbue it with new life. But instead of erasing that past, he had only added another ugly chapter to it.

Perhaps the place was cursed, just like the dark Victorian piles that occupied the gothic novels of his youth. Last night, he dreamt he went, not to Manderley, but back to the Traven house that would haunt him always

"You never did answer my question." Freddie, drawing him out of his reverie.

"The question," Tree said.

"I asked you why you kept the money."

Tree didn't say anything for a time. The cool wind that produced the mist increased in intensity so that the façade appeared to shimmer amid swirling ashes.

"I'm not certain myself," he said finally.

"That's not much of an answer."

"Maybe it had something to do with taking a souvenir—you know, like Comanche warriors used to take scalps to mark their conquests."

"Stealing worthless Tajikistan currency is marking your conquest?"

"Or maybe it had something to do with temptation," Tree continued. "Maybe it was my way of giving into temptation—without really giving into it."

"But you still took the money, Tree. You told a lot of people you didn't have something that in fact you had."

"I know," Tree said. "Part of why I'm changing things. I don't like what the job is doing to me."

"No doubt about it," Freddie said. "I prefer the former *Sun-Times* reporter, the guy I met at that Gold Coast dinner party, the delightful character I fell in love with despite myself. I've never been so sure about the Sanibel Sunset Detective."

"I know that," Tree said. "The *Sun-Times* reporter is gone, and he's not coming back, as much as I'd like him to. And now I'm getting rid of the Sanibel Sunset Detective, too."

"So who does that leave?" Freddie asked.

Tree thought about it a moment before he said, "Maybe the aging, crippled, shot-up old fool who loves you more than anything else in the world."

Freddie reached out and took his hand. "Then that's more than enough."

When they reached the gate, Tree looked back at the house, and he couldn't see it anymore. They got in the Mercedes. Freddie started up the engine. Elvis was on the radio.

Acknowledgments

Shortly after he began touring again in 1970, Elvis Presley came to Detroit's Olympia Stadium. That's where I first saw him in person—September 11, 1970, to be exact.

That concert was a surreal experience. Elvis even then was a mythic figure, a mystery unavailable to the public for thirteen years except on the screen in a series of mostly awful movies. Now here he was in person, glowing in white on stage, delivering an electric performance for forty-five minutes. Elvis lived—right there in front of us.

I saw him twice more after that, in 1972, again in Detroit, and then years later in June 1976 in Buffalo. Since his death in August 1977, there has been lots of talk about how the level of his performance deteriorated, but none of that deterioration was evident in the concerts I attended. He was Elvis, the King, and, on the occasions I saw him, he did nothing but please his ecstatic audience.

Passing time has only reinforced the Elvis mythology to the point where it once again is hard to imagine he really existed, except as part of our pop cultural dreams—dreams shared by Baby Boomers who still flock to Graceland, Elvis's home in Memphis, now a tourist attraction; listen to the all-Elvis station on satellite radio; and keep hundreds of Elvis impersonators gainfully employed.

Whether a younger generation shares the same fascination with him as their aging elders, is debatable. The Beatles transcend time, their bright pop tunes forming the basis for much of today's music. But Elvis, his roots deep in the South of rockabilly and rhythm and blues, tends to get lost in our collective past. The white jump suits probably don't help.

Still, for those of us of a certain age, Elvis remains a magical, haunting presence. I thought a lot about him as I wrote *The Two Sanibel Sunset Detectives*. There is something so powerful about American icons like Elvis and, in previous novels, Hemingway and John Wayne, that I can't resist coming back to them, luxuriating in the mystery of their hold on us so long after their deaths.

I had a great deal of help straightening out my thoughts about Elvis and fitting him into the context of a fourth Tree Callister adventure. I cannot say enough about my wife, Kathy, who acts as First Reader and unswerving supporter. Twenty years my darling, and I love you more than ever.

A team of editors tortures me with the kind of logic and insight that lays bare my many shortcomings and forces me to rewrite a better novel than I ever imagined. Thanks as always to three very tough guys: David Kendall, Ray Bennett, and Bob Burt.

More thanks to my brother Ric Base, the real-life president of the Sanibel-Captiva Chamber of Commerce, a combination publisher, partner, book designer, distributor, confidant, and great pal. Also thanks to my sister-in-law, Alicia, who in addition to patiently putting up with me when I'm in Florida, this time pitched in to read the galleys and also provided background on the Sanibel School. I should hasten to add that any mistakes are those of her brother-in-law. My other sister-in-law, Alexandra Lenhoff, also swung into action, and helped with the galleys, spotting errors the rest of us missed.

My niece, Lindsay Base, provided not only the basis for the book's Nurse Lindsay, but also helped with details about life at Lee Memorial Hospital. My daughter Erin and